Adultery & Other Choices

Other books by Andre Dubus

Adultery &
Other Choices

NINE SHORT STORIES AND A NOVELLA

ANDRE DUBUS

David R. Godine, Publisher
BOSTON

First edition published in 1977 by
David R. Godine, Publisher, Inc.
Post Office Box 450
Jaffrey, New Hampshire 03452
www.godine.com

ISBN: 0-87923-284-6
LC: 77-78392

ACKNOWLEDGEMENTS
"An Afternoon with the Old Man" and "Andromache" first appeared in *The New Yorker;* "Contrition" in *The North American Review;* "Cadence," "Adultery," and "The Bully" in *The Sewanee
Review* (© 1974, 1975, 1977 by the University of the South,
reprinted by permission of the editor); "Graduation" in *The New
Dawn Magazine;* "The Shooting" in *The Carleton Miscellany* (© 1974
by Carleton College); and "Corporal of Artillery" in *Ploughshares.*

Sixth printing, 2010
Printed in the United States of America

To my mother
& in memory of my father

Contents

Unless a man has something stronger, something superior to all outside influences, he only needs to catch a bad cold to lose his balance entirely, to take every bird for a fowl of ill omen, and to hear the baying of the hounds in every noise, while his pessimism or his optimism, together with all his thoughts, great and small, are significant solely as symptoms and in no other way.
—Anton Chekhov, 'A Dull Story'

PART ONE

An Afternoon
with the Old Man

NOW SUNDAY was over, and Paul Clement lay in bed in his room and wished for Marshall, his one wish in all the world right now (and he was a boy with many wishes; 'If wishes were horses beggars would ride,' his mother said when people wished). But Marshall was in Baton Rouge; he had not seen her since the Clements moved from there to Lafayette after the second grade. Maybe he would never see her again. But he would. When he was old enough to drive a car, he would go to Baton Rouge and surprise her. She would squeal and hug him. He saw her, sixteen years old, running down her front steps and sidewalk to meet him; she had breasts and used lipstick and she wore a white dress. Paul knew that now, at ten, he was good-looking—his face was his only pride, it was why Marshall had been his girl—and when he was sixteen he would be even more handsome and bigger and stronger, too, because he had been praying every night and at mass for God to make him an athlete.

He met Marshall in the second grade, a brown-eyed tomboy; she hated dresses, she got dirty when she played, and she brought two cap pistols and a dump truck to the scrap-iron pile at school. ('We sold the Japs our scrap iron, and now they're using it against us,' his father said.) Once at recess she drove away with rocks fat Warren, who was kicking dust at Paul. There was a girl named Penny, with long black hair; she sat behind him in class and handed him pictures she drew (he remembered one of her father lying in bed with a broken leg, the leg suspended and weights hanging from it). Penny was prettier than Marshall, but she sometimes irritated him because she always wanted to hold his hand while they waited in line to go into school, and when there was a movie at school she held him captive, pulling him down the auditorium aisle and into a seat beside her, and during the movie her head was warm on his shoulder, her long hair tickling his throat and damp where it pressed his cheek. So he loved Marshall more. His sisters, Amy and Barbara, and his mother knew about Marshall, but his father did not. When Paul told his mother, she said 'Aren't you going to tell Daddy you have a girl friend?'

'No.'

'You should talk more with Daddy. He loves y'all very much, but he doesn't know how to talk to children.'

His mother said she would keep his secret. One warm afternoon after school he was to go to a birthday party at a girl's house. His mother asked if Marshall would be there, and he said yes. She smiled and combed his hair with her fingers. 'Now don't you kiss her,' she said, in her tease voice.

At the party, they played hide-and-seek, and he and Marshall sat on a running board in the garage; the boy who was It passed by without looking in. The lawn and garage were quiet now; the game had passed them, and Marshall said, 'Kiss me.'

'No.'

'Please.' She had olive skin, her brown eyes were large, and a front tooth was missing.

'If you close your eyes,' he said. She did, and he kissed her lips and tasted the line of sweat above her mouth.

After hide-and-seek, Marshall and Paul got on the swing hanging from an oak. Marshall wanted him to sit; she stood facing him, her feet squeezed between his hips and the ropes, her skirt moving against his face as she pumped them higher and higher till they swung up level with the branch where the ropes were tied, and she said, 'I'd like to go *all* around, over the branch.' Paul hoped she wouldn't try.

When he got home his mother asked if he kissed Marshall and he said yes. She smiled and hugged him.

Here in Lafayette he did not have a girl. He did not even know a girl his age, because he didn't go to a public school now; he went to Cathedral, a boys' school taught by Christian Brothers. At the school in Baton Rouge there had been recess, but no one told you what to play and usually he had been with Penny or Marshall, mostly Marshall. But at Cathedral there was physical education for an hour every day, and it was like being in Baton Rouge when his father still played with them, throwing a tennis ball in the back yard. If Barbara or Amy threw to Paul he sometimes caught it and sometimes did not, but when his father threw it or even if his father was just watching, his muscles stiffened and his belly fluttered and he always missed. At Cathedral it was like that, like being watched by his father.

His father had not played golf in Baton Rouge, or for the first two years in Lafayette; then a priest named Father O'Gorman started coming over and eating supper with them. In summer before supper the men drank beer on the screen porch and listened to the six-o'clock news. Father O'Gorman was a bulky man who always smelled like cigars; he liked to tousle Paul's hair. He told Paul's mother not to worry that her husband was an Episcopalian and didn't go to church. 'Any man who kneels down and says his prayers every night the way your husband does is a good man.' That is what Father O'Gorman told her; she told it to Paul, who had not worried about his father going to hell until the day his mother said the priest said he would not.

Father O'Gorman got Paul's father interested in golf. Soon he had clubs and a bag and shoes, and was taking lessons, playing every Saturday and Sunday, and practicing two or three times a week after work and sometimes on Saturday mornings. One night at supper Paul's mother said to Father O'Gorman, 'If I run off with another man it'll be your fault, Father.' She was smiling the way she did when she didn't see anything funny. 'My husband and I used to be together every weekend, now I'm all by myself.'

Paul had not liked those weekends very much. On many Sundays they had gone to New Iberia to visit his mother's family, the Kelleys, who had once had money and lived in a big brick house with Negro women working inside and Negro men working in a yard as big as a school ground, but later all the money was gone and the house, too, and the married aunts and uncles lived like the Clements in small white houses on quiet streets. Those drives to New Iberia were quiet; once there, though, his parents had drinks, and on the way home there was talking.

'I'm home every night,' his father said. 'She knows that.'

'Well, sure you're home, when it's too dark to see the ball, and all your cronies and Betsy Robichaux have gone home, so there's nobody to drink your old beer with.' She was smiling at Paul's father, and winking at Father O'Gorman.

Paul's father practiced on a school ground near their house, and he wanted Paul to shag balls for him. The pay was fifty cents, and it was an easy job to stand daydreaming with a canvas bag in his hand and watch his father's small faceless figure, the quick pencil-small flash of swinging golf club, and then spot the ball in the air and stay clear of it till it struck the ground. Easy enough, and he liked earning the money. But he did not like to shag balls, for it wasn't simply a job like raking leaves. He was supposed to like picking up balls that his father hit; afterward, in the car, he was supposed to be interested while his father explained the different irons and woods, and told why sometimes he sliced and sometimes hooked. And he was supposed to want to caddie, to spend all Sunday afternoon following his father around the golf course. 'Maybe you'll want to caddie one of these Sundays,' his father said as they drove home from the school ground. 'I know you can't miss the Saturday picture show, but maybe Sundays—keeps the money in the family that way.' Paul sat stiffly, looking through the windshield, smelling the leather golf bag and his father's sweat. 'Maybe so,' he said.

Now tonight if Marshall were here with him, and if for some reason his parents and Amy and Barbara left the house and went someplace, like visiting in New Iberia, he and Marshall would go to the kitchen and he would make peanut-butter and blackberry-preserve sandwiches. They would take them with glasses of cold milk to the living room, where the large lazy-sounding oscillating floor fan moved the curtain at one end of its arc, then rustled the Sunday paper on the couch as it swept back. He would sit beside her on the couch, and when they finished the sandwiches he would rest his head in her lap and look up at her bright eyes and tell her about today, how at Sunday dinner his father had said, 'Want to come out today?' and he had chewed a large bite of chocolate cake, trying to think of a reason not to, and then swallowed and said, 'Sure.'

· 4 ·

After dinner, his father got an extra pack of Luckies from the bedroom, and then it was time to go. His mother walked out on the screen porch with them; the wisteria climbing the screen was blooming lavender. 'Keep an eye on him in this heat,' she said to his father.

'I will.'

She kissed them. As they walked to the car, she called, 'Look at my two handsome men. Paul, be a good influence on your father, bring him home early.'

In the car, they did not talk for six blocks or so. Then his father told him he ought to have a cap to keep the sun off his head, and Paul said he'd be O.K.

'That mama of yours, if I bring you home with a headache she'll say the golf course is the only place the sun shines.'

Paul smiled. The rest of the way to the golf course, they did not talk. Walking to the clubhouse, Paul trailed a step or two behind his father. Caddies stood near the sidewalk—tall boys with dirty bare feet or ragged sneakers and hard brown biceps. Several of them were smoking. ('It stunts the growth,' his mother said.) They were the kind of boys Paul always yielded the sidewalk to when he walked to the cowboy show and serial in town on Saturdays. Paul looked out at the golf course, shielding his eyes with one hand, and studied the distant greens and fairways as he and his father passed the boys and their smell of cigarette smoke and sweat and sweet hair oil.

'Mr. Clement, you need a caddie?'

'No thanks, Tujack. I got my boy.'

From under his shielding hand, Paul stared over the flat fairway at a tiny red flag, hanging limply over the heat shimmer. As he followed his father into the clubhouse, he felt their eyes on him; then, turning a corner around the showcase of clubs, he was out of their vision, and he followed his father's broad shoulders and brown hairy arms into the locker room. His father sat on a bench and put on his golf shoes.

'That Tujack's going to be a hell of a golfer.'

'He plays?'

'They all play, these caddies.'

Outside, in the hot dust behind the clubhouse, his father strapped the golf bag onto a cart, and Paul pulled it behind him to the first tee. Tujack was there, a tall wiry boy of about sixteen, a golf bag slung over his shoulder. Paul shook hands with Mr. Blanchet, Mr. Voorhies, Mr. Peck. Each of them, as he shook hands, looked Paul up and down, as though to judge what sort of boy their friend had. Paul gave his father the driver and then pulled the cart away from the tee, stopping short of the three caddies, who stood under a sycamore. He was the only one using a cart, and he wished his father hadn't done that. I can carry it, he wanted to say.

The first hole had a long dogleg going to the left around a field of short brown weeds. His father shot first, driving two-thirds of the way down the first leg; he came over and gave Paul the driver and stood between him and the caddies, closing the distance. 'You'll be on in two, Mr. Clement,' Tujack said.

'You could, Tujack. Not me.'

They were quiet while the others shot, and then Paul walked beside his father, pulling the cart behind him. It seemed badly balanced, and he watched the ground ahead of him for those small rises that might tip the cart over on its side with a shamefaced clanking of clubs. After the first nine, they stopped at the clubhouse for a drink, and his father asked him how he was holding up. 'Fine,' Paul said. He was. He didn't tire on the second nine, either. It was a hot afternoon, but he liked to sweat, and there was not much need for talking. ('Good shot.' 'Well, let's see what I can do with the brassie.') Usually, between shots, he walked a little to the rear, and his father talked to one of the men.

When they finished playing, his father gave him a dollar and a quarter and told him he was a good caddie, then asked if he was tired or too hot and what did he want to drink, and took him into the clubhouse and up to the counter. 'Give this boy a Grapette and some cheese crackers,' his father said, his hand coming down on Paul's shoulder, staying there.

'That your boy?' the man behind the counter said.

'That's him,' the hand on Paul's shoulder squeezing now, rocking him back and forth. Paul lowered his eyes and smiled and blushed, just as he did each time his father said, 'I'd like you to meet my boy,' his father smiling, mussing his hair, Paul shaking the large extended hand, squeezing it ('Always squeeze,' his mother told him. 'Don't give someone a dead fish'). 'He's got a good grip,' one man had said, and for a moment Paul had been proud.

Now his father was drinking beer with his friends—what Paul's mother called the nineteenth hole. Paul liked watching him have fun, pouring the good summer-smelling beer in his glass, laughing, talking about the game they just played and other games they had played. They talked about baseball, too; a team called the Dodgers was going to have a colored boy playing this year. Betsy Robichaux and another woman came to their table, and the four men and Paul stood up; Mr. Peck got two chairs from the next table. Paul squeezed the women's hands, too, but not quite as hard.

'He's got his daddy's looks,' Betsy Robichaux said.

His father grinned and his blue eyes twinkled. She was not really pretty but she was nice-looking, Paul thought. She sat opposite him with her back to the window that ran the length of the clubhouse, so he watched her, caught himself staring at her now and then, but most of the time he remembered to pretend he was looking past her at the eighteenth green, where long-shadowed men leaned on putters. She was deeply tanned and slender. Her voice was husky, she laughed a lot, she said hell and damn, and she was always smoking a Pall Mall, gesturing with it in her ringless left hand. Paul knew she was not a lady like his mother, but he liked watching women smoke, for a cigarette made them somehow different, like women in movies instead of mothers. She sat there talking golf with the men, and Paul knew his father liked talking golf with her better than with his mother, who only pretended she was interested (Paul could tell by her voice). But thinking about his mother made him feel guilty, as though he were betraying his father, as though he were his mother's spy, recording every time his father said 'Betsy.' He decided to count the beers his father drank, so if his mother said something Paul could defend him.

His father drank five beers (Paul had two Grapettes and two packages of cheese crackers with peanut butter), and then it was dusk and they drove home, his father talking all the way in his drinking voice, relaxed, its tone without edges now, rounded by some quality that was almost tenderness, almost affection. He talked golf. Sometimes, when he paused, Paul said yes. As they approached the corner of their street, his father reached over and lightly slapped Paul's leg, then gave it a squeeze.

'Well,' he said. 'It's not so bad to spend an afternoon with the old man, is it?'

'Nope,' Paul said, and knew at once how that sounded, how his father must have heard only their failure in that one little word, because how could his father possibly know, ever forever know, that even that one word had released so much that tears came to his eyes, and it was as if his soul wanted to talk and hug his father but his body could not, and all he could do was in silence love his father as though he were a memory, as the afternoon already was a memory.

His mother met them on the screen porch. 'Did my two men have fun together?'

'Sure we did. He's a good caddie.'

'Did you have fun?' she asked Paul.

He took a quick deep breath, closed his mouth tightly, pressed a finger under his nose, and pretended to hold back a sneeze as he walked past her.

Now in his bed he grew sleepy to the sound of the fan. He wondered if they would have a new car when he was a big boy. He saw the car as a blue one, and it smelled new inside. Now Marshall came out in her white dress and kissed him in the evening sun right there on her front steps; she had the line of sweat over her lips and smelled of perfume. Holding hands, they walked to the car. Her head came to about his shoulder; just before he opened the car door, she put her hand on his bicep and squeezed it. Her face was lovely and sad for him. 'I'm glad you're taking me,' she said.

In the car, she slid close to him. Her arms were dark against the lap of her dress. He offered his pack of Luckies, and they lit them from the dashboard lighter. They drove out of town, then on a long road through woods. The road started climbing and they came out above the woods at trimmed bright grass and spreading live oaks, and in their shade old tombstones and crosses. They left the car and very quietly, holding hands, they walked in the oak shade to his father's grave. He made the sign of the cross, bowed his head, and prayed for his father's soul. When Marshall saw the tears in his eyes, she put her arm around his waist and hugged him tightly while he prayed.

Contrition

AFTER SCHOOL Paul and Eddie walked fast; it was a cold January day, the sky had been growing darker all afternoon, and they could feel rain coming on the wind. They crossed themselves as they passed the Cathedral; then they were walking by the Bishop's huge house, with its iron fence; on his lawn pines and live oaks thrashed in the wind.

'I'm going to learn an instrument,' Eddie said.

Paul looked up at him, and then at the cars driving with their lights on. The whole town seemed to be hurrying home before the winter rain. He thought of Eddie going to a woman's house and taking piano lessons and at the end of the year playing in a recital, taking his turn among girls in velveteen dresses with barrettes in their hair.

'I talked to Brother Eugene yesterday.'

'You didn't tell me.'

'I thought about it during vacation, and I talked to my folks about it.'

'You'd take lessons at school? And be in the band?'

'I couldn't be in the band for a while. It's mostly just high school boys. But maybe by the eighth grade.'

Eddie was walking faster, looking up at the sky and the trees blowing above the rooftops. In the third grade, when they had both entered Cathedral, Paul had chosen Eddie as his friend. Paul was short and thin and often pressed a handkerchief to his sniffling hayfevered nose. Eddie was taller, but like Paul he moved with caution among the other boys, his voice seemed bent on silencing itself, and his gestures were close to his body as though apologizing for the space he occupied. At recess he and Eddie drank Cokes together, and on the athletic field they watched each other's failures. Paul believed they could endure grammar school together and by the time they reached high school they would change or the world would change. He did not know precisely how. At Cathedral the boys started in the third grade and went through the twelfth and sometimes when he thought of that he saw himself and Eddie unchanged and outcast until finally they crossed the stage wearing caps and gowns. But most of the time he believed when they reached high school the days would no longer cost so much of fear and patience and hope.

'We better hurry,' Eddie said, and started to run. They were a block from his house when the rain fell hard and cold, and their faces dripped and they shivered as they stomped into the kitchen where Mrs. Kirkpatrick was moving toward the door, wearing an overcoat and scarf.

'I was just going to get you,' she said, and kissed Eddie. Susan was sitting at the table, and she was smoking. 'Paul, you'd better call your mother and tell her I'll take you home. We'll have hot chocolate.' She hugged Eddie. Paul hung his jacket on a hook by the door and, rubbing his hair with his handkerchief, he secretly watched Susan who was sixteen and pretty, with hair that was light brown, almost blonde, the color of Eddie's, and bright red lips and fingernails. He watched her inhaling, and he tingled with guilt and delightful fascination for the secret and forbidden. One Saturday afternoon as Paul and Eddie were walking home after a Red Ryder movie Eddie said he had gone upstairs yesterday and found Susan and his mother smoking in Susan's room and they had told him not to tell his father because he would be hurt. Eddie told this with the worried, conspiratorial tone of someone confiding a sin. Now here was Susan, and he looked at her brown Philip Morris pack on the table and the cigarette in her hands, then he moved through the kitchen, into the hall, toward the phone.

In the Kirkpatrick house there seemed to be only the one secret, and it was kept from Eddie's father in a lovingly collusive way, like a gift. Eddie had said he told his father about everything that bothered him: how unhappy he was at school when they had to play football and then basketball and then softball. In Paul's house everyone was a secret. One Saturday evening last summer his parents had gone out; it was twilight when they left and Paul was in the back yard; he was lying under the fig tree, pretending he was the last Marine alive on Wake Island, when he heard the car doors slam and the engine start. He crawled out from under the tree and ran around to the front yard, to the driveway, but they were gone, they were at the end of the block, and he watched the tail lights as his father braked and then drove on. His sisters were inside the house but he did not go in. He went back to the fig tree and lay under it, in the darkness and sadness under the wide leaves. Always before his parents went out they kissed him and his sisters. Now he lay unkissed, and thinking of the back of the car as it drove away he began to cry. In the sweet luxury of tears he pressed his face into the grass until he heard the back door close. He lay quietly. In the pale dying light Barbara came across the lawn; she approached him and walked past the tree and stood with her back to him. She was looking up at the sky. Then he saw that she was crying. At first she cried quietly, but then she began to moan and sob. Finally she wiped her face with her hands and went sniffing past him and into the house. He waited a while then left his tree, his tears, his foxhole; from the top of the tree a mockingbird screamed at him.

The memory of Barbara that summer night was pleasurably mysterious, and often when he thought of her he saw her weeping at the sky. There were other memories he kept in his heart like old photographs. His father rarely talked at home, but when friends came for drinks Paul lay on his bed and listened to the drone of the women at one end of the room and the loud talk of the men at the other and, above it all, his father. He heard his father tell stories about when he was first married and he was a surveyor for the utilities company he still worked for; now he was a district manager. His father had worn a holstered .22 Colt Woodsman and shot cottonmouths in the rice fields. Once one of the crew caught a king snake and carried it in a paper bag until they found a cottonmouth; he threw the king snake on it and the crew watched the fight; listening to his father's voice through the wall he could see the twining snakes and the cottonmouth's slow death. A man who owned the land they were surveying told his father to get off and said his company was nothing but a bunch of crooked sons of bitches anyway and his father knocked him down. Once they had to deal with a Negro and when the talking was done the Negro offered his hand and his father took it. In the car one of the crew said: You shook his hand. His father said: And if I hadn't, *then* who would have been the gentleman?

His father often said children should be seen and not heard and at times it seemed that Paul's silence made him invisible too and he could listen like a spy. On an afternoon last summer he sat petting his yellow dog Mike. He sat on the bottom step of the back porch and his father and mother sat on the top step. His father had finished mowing the lawn and Paul smelled his sweat and the beer he was drinking and the smell of clean dog and freshly cut grass; Mike turned on his back and grinned while Paul scratched his belly. Above Paul his parents were murmuring, and with his fingers on Mike's ribs he concentrated all of himself into one ear, and the muted sound of their voices became words.

'I'm afraid to,' his mother said.

'We can use rubbers.'

'Don't talk that way.'

He heard his father's Zippo, then smelled the smoke. It was all he smelled in the air now. His father and mother sat quietly behind him.

When he returned to the kitchen from calling his mother, Mrs. Kirkpatrick was stirring chocolate on the stove. They were drinking it when the front door opened; Susan put her cigarettes in her purse and Mr. Kirkpatrick came in; he was a slender, gentle man whose posture was slightly stooped. He greeted them all and spoke of the rain and tousled Eddie's hair, then made himself a drink and joined them at the table.

'I told Paul I'm going to take an instrument.'

'What do you think of that, Paul?'

Mine's better, he thought, looking at Mr. Kirkpatrick's kind brown eyes with crinkled corners and seeing his father's ruddy face and blue eyes and thin wavy hair, nearly black now though his mother said when she met him it was blond curls; seeing his father's broad shoulders and deep hairy chest and hairy arms and hearing the gruff voice; he was shy with all fathers, he went each year in dread to the Rotary father and son luncheon where, in turn, he had to stand on a chair and speak his name to the upturned faces; yet he wasn't shy with Mr. Kirkpatrick, he felt with him now the stirrings of relief, felt drawn to him as though by trust and love, and he wanted to say: *Music is for sissies;* he wanted to say: *Susan smokes;* he wanted to say: *I could beat up Eddie;* and he wanted to show them he could.

'I guess it's all right,' he said.

'You should do it too,' Susan said. 'Y'all could learn together.'

'Maybe I will,' he said.

Next day the sun and a cold wind dried the earth and after school Paul and Eddie talked to Brother Eugene. He was tall and kept pushing his glasses up on his nose, and his black robe smelled of chalk dust where he had wiped his hands. They told him they wanted to learn the trumpet but he said they should take the French horn. He took them up the wooden stairs to the second floor and unlocked the bandroom and showed them a French horn. He said if they learned to play it they could easily play the trumpet and cornet as well; but they should learn the French horn because the band had all the trumpet players it needed for years to come but soon there would be a shortage of French horns. If they worked hard they could start playing in the regular band in two years when they were only in the seventh grade; they would wear uniforms and go on band trips to play at football games and they would march in the homecoming parade and Mardi Gras parade and many colleges gave band scholarships. He raised the horn to his lips and blew a series of notes.

When Paul got home he told his mother and sisters. Amy said Maybe he'd be a famous trumpet player like Harry James, Barbara said It might be nice and his mother said It was very exciting but they would have to wait and see what Daddy said. She made cinammon toast and a pot of tea and they all sat at the kitchen table. When his father came home Paul listened through the closed kitchen door to him and Mike. From windows he had watched Mike greeting his father as he emerged from his car, his father's near-scowling face suddenly laughing as the dog ran to him and leaped up at him, his father crouching and pushing Mike back with gentle slaps, Mike growling and wagging his tail and barking, jumping again and again to his father's hands and loving voice. Now in the living room they were laughing and growling, and they came into the kitchen, Mike following through the swinging door, and his father's sweeping glance quizzical in the silence which he then broke with hello, kissed Paul's mother, poured bourbon and water, and went to the living room to read the evening paper.

Usually at supper his mother and sisters talked about school and the nuns or a dress his mother was making for one of them or about other things that Paul paid no attention to while he ate. But that night they were quiet and he knew they were waiting for him. Mike came to watch them and his father said: 'Mike, you know better than that. Go back to the living room. Go on.'

Mike went back and lay on the rug, watching them.

'Paul?' his mother said. 'Did anything new happen at school today?'

Paul looked at her urging brown eyes. Then his father said: 'Why should anything new happen?'

Watching his mother he saw that the question was to her.

'I don't know,' his mother said. 'It can't be the same *every* day.'

Barbara was watching him. He looked at her and said: 'It's pretty much the same every day.'

When they finished eating, his father took a piece of ham to the living room and dropped it between Mike's paws.

That night Paul lay in the dark in his room adjacent to the living room and listened to them through the wall. He knew it was eleven o'clock because his father had finished reading. Every week he read *The Saturday Evening Post*, *Time*, *Collier's*, *The Reader's Digest*, *Life*, and a mystery or a book by a golf pro. While he read Mike slept beside his chair and now and then his father's hand lowered, with stroking fingers, to Mike's head. At eleven o'clock he slept.

'Paul wants to take the French horn.'

'Where's he going to take it? To the picture show?'

'He's serious about it.'

'Who, him? Who talked him into it?'

'Nobody did. Eddie's going to start, and they've talked it over, but I'm sure Eddie didn't—'

'Ah: Eddie. When was all this?'

'Today.'

'Today. All of a sudden he's a musician. Did you ever hear that boy say he wanted to be a musician till now?'

'Well there has to be a first day for everything.'

'Why didn't he tell me himself? Is that what all that monkey business was about at supper?'

'He was afraid to.'

'Afraid to? Did he tell you that?'

'No, he—'

'Did he ask you to ask me?'

'No, I just—'

'Why is my son afraid of me? Can you tell me that? I've spanked that boy three times in ten years. What's he afraid of?'

'He's very sensitive.'

'Sensitive. If he's so sensitive why doesn't he know—Never mind: do they have the horns at school?'

'You have to buy one.'

'Buy one.'

'Or mabe rent one.'

'Or maybe rent one. Goddamn.'

'It means a lot to him. He'll be in the high school band. Maybe he can get a college scholarship.'

'Goddamn,' his father said.

At breakfast his father was reading the paper. Paul waited. He had finished his oatmeal and milk and toast, the girls had gone to brush their teeth, his mother was putting the dishes in the sink, and finally he rose to leave too when his father lowered the paper and looked at him.

'What's this your mother tells me about a French horn?'

The blue eyes were gazing into his and he could see in them the silence when he and his father were trapped together in a car, and the relief he felt at all his father's departures and the fear at his arrivals.

'I decided not to,' Paul said. 'It costs too much.'

'Wait a minute: that's not what I asked. Do you want to play the horn?'

'I guess so.'

'Son, I can buy a horn; I can borrow for that. Do you or don't you want to learn to play it.'

'Yesterday you wanted to,' his mother said, and he looked at her. She quickly nodded her head, then gestured with it toward his father, then nodded again. In one of his frequent daydreams he was captured by a band of amazons and taken to a tropical island where they lived; they were tall and lovely and they fed him and cared for him and he could not leave. There was some threatening yet attractive mystery about them too, as if they all shared a secret and it had to do with him; perhaps one morning they would tie him to an altar and sacrifice him to the sun; his heart plucked out, his soul would rise above the beautiful women. He wished he were with them now.

'Yes, I'd like to.' he said.

'All right,' his father said, the paper rising into place again; then from behind it he muttered: 'Why didn't you say so.'

Paul stood there until he was sure his father was reading again and was not waiting for an answer.

Twice a week Paul and Eddie arrived at school carrying their cased horns bumping against their legs and in the afternoon, after an hour's lesson, walked home with them. Paul was a victim of newspaper and magazine cartoons. Why hadn't he'd thought of the *size* of the horn? In cartoons only the inept carried large instruments, usually tubas, and their practicing made cats and dogs howl, neighbors shout, close windows, throw old shoes. Now when he walked home carrying the horn, he was no longer anonymous: anyone driving by could see what he was. After supper he went to his room and closed the door and tried to play the notes. The horn was silver with a shiny brass bell and holding it and depressing its valves smelling of oil he wished he could give it the love it deserved. His father had brought it home and opened the case on the dining room table and displayed for Paul and his sisters and mother the horn nestled in red felt. A hundred dollars, he said; I hope it's worth it. Oh let's don't talk about money, Paul's mother said; I hate the dirty old stuff. Two days later Eddie's father bought a used horn, a gold one with two dents on the bell, and Paul felt deceived.

Sitting in his room he looked at the notes on the page; they made no sense to him. He began to hate the notes themselves, the way they sat inscrutable and arrogant on the stern bars which he didn't understand either. At times he thought he was simply stupid; he would have preferred that to the truth which sometimes surfaced in his mind: that while he and Eddie sat before Brother Eugene tapping the music sheets with his baton, tapping their horns with his baton, sometimes tapping their knuckles and hands with his baton, Paul was not there: he watched himself looking at the notes; he listened to himself trying to blow them; and all the time he was in suspension, waiting. He was waiting for something to happen. One afternoon he would all at once love the horn, he would know and love the notes, and his lips would blow sweet silver. Or one day someone would steal his horn. Or the school would burn to the ground or Brother Eugene would drop dead.

On the first night he practiced at home his father said it sounded like a bullfrog. Paul said it was hard to get the lips right. He played every night for the first two weeks, making sounds that had nothing to do with the notes he glared at on the sheet, wanting to cross them out with a pencil, to gouge them with its point. For the first time in his life he was living a public lie. With his father he had lived a lie for as long as he could remember: he believed his father wanted him to be popular and athletic at school, so Paul never told him about his days. But now the lie had spread: it touched his mother and Amy and Barbara and Brother Eugene and even Eddie. He hated the lie, not for its sin but for its isolation; and every Tuesday and Thursday he carried the horn to school as though it were a dead bird; and in the afternoons he climbed the stairs with Eddie to the band room and to Brother Eugene's growing impatience; then entering his house he put the horn on the closet floor, wanting to kick it, and at supper he answered questions about his music lessons. After two weeks of practicing at home his father asked him, the gruff voice trying to be gentle and bantering, if he'd practice when he came home from school, not at night. As lovely as the French horn is, his father said, it wasn't meant to accompany reading.

Nor was anything else. When his father came home in the evenings Amy took her records off the record player. After supper, except during the Sunday night radio shows, the living room was quiet. If friends of Amy or Barbara came over they went to the girls' bedroom and closed the door. The phone was in the hall and when Paul talked to Eddie at night he turned his back to the living room and spoke in a low, furtive voice. Lying in bed he could hear Mike scratching a flea, his father returning one magazine to the rack and getting another, his mother yawning in the chair where she read. But he was grateful for that silence resting on his horn too. He started practicing before his father came home; but if his mother was shopping or playing bridge he put the horn away and when she came home and asked if he had practiced he said yes. He saw the end coming.

He did not know how it would come, and when it did he felt betrayed again: Eddie phoned Paul on a Wednesday night and said he wasn't going to the lesson tomorrow, he was quitting.

'I haven't enjoyed it very much,' Eddie said. 'Have you?'

'I don't know. It hasn't been so bad.'

'I've hated it. I don't like the French horn. It's big and clumsy and I don't like the sound. I wish now I had taken the clarinet. Daddy says Brother Eugene used us, he talked us into the French horn so he'd have some for the band. He says if I want to take the clarinet after a while I can get lessons from somebody in town.'

'What about the horn? What are you going to do with the horn?'

'He'll sell it back to the store.'

The phone was outside his sisters' room. Barbara had been reading on the bed she shared with Amy; now she was watching him. When he hung up she said: 'Eddie quit, didn't he.'

'Yes.'

'What are you going to do now?'

'I don't know.'

'Why don't you quit?'

He shrugged.

'Just tell Daddy you've tried it and you don't like it. He can sell the horn. Paul: what are you going to do—take those silly lessons till you're twenty-one years old?'

Next day he went to his lesson. Without Eddie, his clumsy hypocrisy filled the room: as Brother Eugene called for a note Paul assumed a look of memory and concentration while his fingers pressed any valves they touched and he blew into the horn. Brother Eugene paced back and forth, turned his back to Paul, then spun to face him.

'Paul, you're not practicing. You've learned nothing in a month. At least when Eddie was with us you could watch his fingers. Why aren't you practicing? Don't you know you owe it to your father? He had to sacrifice to buy that horn. It's a beautiful horn. If you have no pride in yourself, can't you at least do that much for your father?'

'He won't let me.'

'What do you mean, he won't let you?'

'He won't let me practice. He likes quiet in the house.'

Brother Eugene tapped the music stand once with his baton then pushed his glasses higher on his nose.

'Maybe I better talk to him,' he said.

'You better not,' Paul said. 'He's Episcopalian, and he doesn't like Brothers. He—'

'He what, Paul?'

'I heard him talking once—he wants to—'

'He wants to what, Paul?'

'He wants to use those things. With my mother.'

He looked down at the horn in his lap. Then he stroked it with his fingers and looked at Brother Eugene's robe and shoes.

'We can stop for today,' Brother Eugene said. 'If you'd like to talk about the other—'

Paul shook his head.

'It's all right,' he said. 'And I can practice in the afternoons. Just there's not much time.'

He took the mouthpiece from the horn and put the horn in its case.

In the kitchen his mother said: 'I never did think that was the right instrument for you. But Daddy will be disappointed.'

'Why should he be?' Barbara said. 'Nobody has to play the French horn.'

'Well, he spent a lot of money on that horn.' She looked at Paul. 'Are you going to tell him? I want you to stand up like a man and tell him yourself.'

'Okay,' he said.

He went out to the back yard. The day was blue and warm and he stood waiting in the sunlight, clinging to the vision of tomorrow when it would all be over, until in the shadows of twilight he heard the slamming of his father's car door and then Mike growling happily. When those sounds stopped he went into the kitchen as his father pushed through its door. His mother was at the stove and Barbara was gone. He looked quickly at his father and said: 'I want to quit the horn.'

'What?' His father still wore his hat, and his overcoat was over his arm. 'You want to *what*?'

'Now don't shout at him,' his mother said.

His father looked at them both, then sighed and shook his head.

'Goddamn,' he said, and went back through the door; he went through it fast and it swung twice behind him before it closed.

'You should have waited till he had his drink. You know I always wait till he's had his drink.'

When his father came back he had taken off his coat and tie and rolled up the cuffs of his white shirt. He was midway across the kitchen toward the liquor cabinet when he stopped and looked at Paul: 'What do you mean, you want to quit? You've only been at it a month! You haven't even *start*ed the Goddamn thing! Why do you want to *quit*?'

Paul shrugged and looked down, then raised his eyes to his father; his father's face was blurred. He blinked and it was clear again and he was too ashamed of the tears on his cheeks to wipe them.

'Goddamnit what are you *cry*ing for. What's he *cry*ing for.' His father stood between them, his fierce clenched jaws now turned to her. '*Why* is he crying! Okay, he wants to quit the Goddamn horn. *Okay*. I can't *make* him play it. He stands there crying. *I'm* the one who borrowed the Goddamn hundred dollars. What'll I do with that horn now, huh?' He looked at Paul. 'Huh? Can you tell me that?'

'We can sell it,' his mother said.

'We can sell it.' His father looked at her. 'That's not even the point. Why in the hell did he ever think he wanted to play the Goddamn thing to begin with? He didn't *ever* want to. It's just something he and the other one, Eddie, dreamed up. When did Eddie quit?'

'I don't know,' his mother said. 'Yesterday. Brother Eugene shouldn't have—'

'The hell with Brother Eugene. What's *he* got to do with it? I pity the poor bastard for wasting his time. With *what*?' Looking at her, he pointed a finger at Paul. 'What's he good for? Not a Goddamn thing. He doesn't do one Goddamn thing but mope around the house, he's not good for one Goddamn thing but to go to cowboy shows and shoot Japs and Indians in the back yard. What the hell else does he do? Huh? What else?—' Paul would not remember the rest. In the explosion of his father's voice he stood with the tears he would not wipe. Once he felt he was kneeling with his head bowed. Finally the sound ended and he left the room and his father's face. He went to his room and lay face-down on his bed and wiped his eyes. Then he lay on his back and looked at the ceiling. Barbara came in and sat on the bed and held his hand. She looked as though she might cry.

'He's terrible,' she said.

In her pink cheeks and blue eyes he saw himself, saw the narrow breadth of his soul which in ten years had learned nothing of courage and so much of lies; to her face and the clasp of her hand he silently asked his father's question—*What's he good for?*—and he could not accept the answer of her gaze and touch, that he was a little brother she loved. Closing his eyes he found no answer there either, in the dark of his mind where memories of himself swam: he saw the day of snow when he was five, the only time in his life he had seen snow and that night it melted; in the afternoon his father came home and threw snowballs at them and one hit Paul in the eye and he cried and his mother said: *You're too rough with him, he's only a little boy;* and he saw the night when he was two and after supper his father picked him up and held him laughing and tossed him in the air and caught him, then again, both of them laughing as his father tossed and tossed while his mother's voice cut through the blur of ceiling and walls and his father's arms and laughing upturned face: *You'll make him sick*, and then he was, in the air, and on the rug as his father lowered him to the floor and her voice started again. Opening his eyes to look at Barbara he murmured: 'No he isn't.'

The Bully

H E DID NOT tell even Eddie about the cat. It was in summer, in August. The Clements were renting a strange house then. It had been built by the owner and a Negro; it was two stories and its brick and cement walls were a foot thick. It was shaped like a box. For some reason no one had ever explained, the owner had dug a basement under the house after it was built; perhaps he could not stop building. A mule had dragged the dirt away, climbing up the steep ramp which later became the driveway. After that the mule died. It was the only basement in town, it was always wet, and there was a sump pump they could hear inside the house when it rained.

It was raining the day Paul found the cat down there, crouched between the car and the wall at the driest side of the basement. It was white with a large brown spot on its left side, and the right forepaw was brown. Paul picked it up and stared into its eyes. When the cat tried to look away Paul held its head. He could feel the cat's heart above his hand; it was beating as fast as his was. Then he walked with it to the pump, walking barefooted in the cool rainwater that ran down the ramp and across the floor. He squatted over the round hole of the pump. Then he thrust the cat's head under water. The cat's legs kicked and reached but Paul's hands were behind its head. Then he was afraid of what he was doing and he put the cat on the floor. It ran under the car and lay watching him. Paul quickly left the basement, walked up the ramp, into the rain. He looked up into the rain at God.

The cat was young, little more than a kitten. An older cat would have been smarter; Paul knew that. But this one stayed. Next morning it gripped the screen door with its front paws and watched the family in the kitchen eating fresh figs on cereal. Amy was eighteen and she had hated all five dogs Paul had lost to cars, age, and sudden disappearance; but she loved cats and when she heard it then saw it she left the table and went outside and picked it up. She stood with the early sunlight on her black hair and held the cat and stroked it and talked to it and it stretched against her breasts.

'I'll give him some milk,' she said through the door.

'Oh no,' his mother said. 'Don't feed strays.'

Barbara went on eating and reading the paper. She was fifteen and smart and plump and she wanted a boy friend and Paul knew she was seldom happy. Paul's father was reading the sports section.

'Come eat before your cereal gets mushy,' his mother said, and Amy came in.

The cat was mewing at the screen again. Paul looked at it and knew if he was alone this morning he would do it, he knew he had to and he wanted to but he faintly hoped someone would stay home and he would be saved. But after his father went to work some girls came in a car and took Amy swimming, his mother went shopping, and Barbara rode her bicycle to a friend's house. In the house alone he felt wicked and he could feel the cat down there in the yard. He went downstairs and into the kitchen. It was on the back porch, a small square of concrete with an iron railing. When the cat heard him it stood on its hind legs and clung to the screen and mewed, and Paul looked at its pink mouth and small pointed teeth.

'Hello, cat,' he said softly.

Then he opened the screen, fast and hard and wide, and slammed the cat against the railing. He stepped out and let the screen shut behind him. The cat was crouched in the corner made by the railing and the brick wall; it watched him; then it looked away and licked its paws. An older cat would have arched its back and prepared to fight or, with a wise and determined face, darted past him. But this one was afraid and uncertain and was now pretending that nothing had happened. When Paul leaned forward and stroked its back it quivered and looked at him. He wished the cat would fight him, would spring at him howling and hissing and clawing. He imagined him and the cat rolling off the concrete steps and onto the ground, fighting. He picked it up and carried it down the back stairs into the basement; all the time he was stroking it. He went to the dark corner where the old clothesline lay on the floor; he picked it up and climbed the stairs again, into the bright sun. He crossed the back yard and went behind the neighbor's garage, where the sycamore tree was. While he slipped the noose over the cat's head the cat was very still. Paul's breath and heart were quick.

Larry Guidry was a short wiry boy with biceps like baseballs, thin curly hair, a small head, and a face the color of housedust. Paul thought his head looked like a cottonmouth's. Larry had no friends but sometimes at recess he joined a group that was joking about girls or parts of girls and when he laughed his eyes were bright. They were bright too when he hurt Paul. In the fifth grade the Brothers had stopped failing him. That was the first year Paul was his classmate. It was, he thought, as if Larry had been waiting for him to catch up. For two years Larry punched his arms, twisted his ears, yanked his hair, and stomped his cold instep as the class waited in line outside of school on winter mornings. Once at supper his mother saw the bruise on his arm and asked him what had happened. He told her a boy hit him. She said he must tell the boy not to do it again, a bruise like that could cause cancer. Did you hit him back? his father said. We were playing, Paul said. Walking home from school in the afternoons and in bed at night Paul fought with Larry, blackened and closed his eyes, broke his nose and jaw, covered his small crinkled face with cuts and blood, and hearing Larry's helpless and defeated pleas, his breast filled as with the brass and bass drum of a passing parade.

Larry came from a poor family. Paul knew this because he came on the school bus from the north end of town and because everything he wore was old: the clean starched and ironed khakis in the fall and spring, the corduroys and sweat shirts and mackinaw in winter, and the black tennis shoes with their soles worn nearly smooth. Paul also believed he had many brothers and sisters. He looked like he came from one of those families. In the summer Larry sold snowballs. He had a roofed, glass-windowed cart attached to the front of his bicycle and he rode about town. Usually he worked the north end where the swimming pool and golf course were and where poor white families lived on the borders of the

Negro section. But sometimes on summer afternoons when Paul and Eddie walked to a movie they saw him on the main street and bought a snowball from him. The three of them spoke nervously and politely, like old schoolmates who hadn't been close. Paul knew Larry wouldn't do anything to them, though he didn't know how he knew it or why it was true: whether because working and bullying didn't go together or because it was summer and bullying was left back there with books and desks and blackboards and ringing bells. I saw Brother Daniel driving somewhere. I saw Louis at the pool. Larry bent over the block of ice, his head and arms inside the cart as he scraped with the hand-scraper; then he packed ice into paper cups and poured over it the flavored syrup. I'll take grape this time. The small hand gave him the cup. He placed a nickel in the palm, his thumb and finger touching the hand.

When Paul went back to school for the seventh grade Larry was sixteen years old, his voice was deeper, but he had not grown; the khakis he wore could have been the same he had worn the autumn before. On the first day of school, about twenty minutes late, Roland Comeaux joined the class. He missed the first bell which summoned the boys to line up in two files facing their teacher, and the second bell which rang usually as the principal, a large, jovial and irascible Frenchman, emerged from the building and stood on the back steps and, with his hands resting on his round belly, looked down at the entire school: the third graders to his left, the high school seniors to his right, and the black-robed Christian Brothers standing with roll books at the head of each column. Brother Gauthier, the seventh-grade teacher, was also from France and he used snuff. In other years Paul had smelled oiled wooden floors, washed blackboards, chalk dust, and the glossy pages of new books. The seventh grade would be the year that smelled of snuff.

Roland Comeaux missed more than the morning line: he missed the morning prayers recited in the classroom, Brother Gauthier leading, each boy standing at his desk, fingering the black rosaries they all carried. Roland came in after they had recited the first decade of the joyful mysteries. They were seated and Larry, sitting behind Paul, had just given his tricep a long hard pinch, and Paul had turned to him a smiling face. When he looked to the front of the class again Roland was coming through the door. He wore khakis and a T-shirt whose sleeves were taut around his veined biceps; in tennis shoes he strode poised and graceful to the desk where he smiled at Brother Gauthier and then, turning, smiled at the class. The smile did not ask for anything. Then he turned back to Brother Gauthier.

At recess that morning the class crowded around the Coke machine, five or six hands at once waiting with a coin at the slot. Paul was toward the rear, holding his nickel in his fist and pocket too, so he didn't see Roland and Wayne until the crowd moved back from the machine with that sudden and quiet shifting that always meant a fight. He could feel the anticipation in their bodies as he squeezed between them and got toward the front. Roland was perhaps an inch taller than Wayne but much lighter; Wayne Landry was short, chubby, and strong, one of the boys the high school football coach waited for.

'Pick it up,' Wayne said.

Then he pushed Roland's chest. In the fights Paul had seen, this pushing was a ritual: boys pushed each other until fear left their eyes, then they fought. Roland did not return Wayne's push. He hit him in the jaw with a left hook (Paul noticed that: not a round-house right but a left, and a hook at that); the second blow was a right to the stomach that would have folded Wayne if it weren't for the left and right which struck almost the same point on his chin. He went to the pavement as though he had slipped on ice. Leaning forward, Paul saw that one outstretched hand lay next to the nickel. Wayne was looking up at Roland, whose fists were unclenched, one hand going into his pocket as he turned to the machine and said: 'I didn't hit your nickel. You dropped it.'

He bought a Coke, opened it, then he bought another. He opened that one and held it down toward Wayne. Wayne sat up and looking at some point past Roland's knees, took it. Roland walked slowly through the crowd of boys. Paul wanted to touch him as he passed. Instead he murmured: 'You looked like Bob Steele.'

The smile Roland turned on him was friendly; Roland's brown

eyes looked into his, as though asking his name.

'Who's Bob Steele?' Roland said.

Then he walked on.

Sometimes on winter afternoons when yesterday's mud was hard footprinted earth, Paul lingered after school and watched the boxers in the gym. He sat with his books in the bleachers and watched Roland in a grey suit skipping rope and then handing the rope to an older boy and crossing the gym where, waiting at the large bag, he talked with a high school boy who fought at a hundred and forty-five pounds. Then Paul watched him working on the bag. The older boy watched too and sometimes spoke to Roland. When the boxers finished in the gym the coach took them for a six-mile run in the cold twilight. Mounting his bicycle Paul watched them leaving. They ran in a formation of two files and Roland, ninety-five pounds and shorter than everyone, ran in front. As Paul pumped past them on the opposite side of the road he could see Roland turning his head, talking to the boy beside him; he was laughing. Paul turned on his light and rode home.

'I don't want to go,' Eddie said. 'I've never been to one.'

'Neither have I,' Paul said.

It was recess, and they stood with hands in their jacket pockets. Paul was looking up at Eddie's face. He liked Eddie's face but sometimes he did not like to be seen with it and now he was thinking of that face at a boxing match. The face showed Eddie's life: good grades, the state of grace, uncertainty about his body in a world of running, pushing, yelling boys, and an imagination that lifted him to other places, other deeds. Looking at Eddie he saw everything he had learned about him in their three years together and he knew that their faces were too much alike and he wished they or at least he had a sneer, a glare, a tightened jaw to show to the world.

'We ought to see Roland anyway,' he said. 'He's fighting first. If we don't like the rest we can leave.'

'Your hero.'

'He's not my *hero*,' thinking of Bob Steele, the quickest fist fighter of all the Saturday cowboys, fading, almost gone, for in the nights now it was Roland he thought of, Roland's quick fists on

Larry's face, and lying in bed it was him merging with the image of Roland, him hitting Larry, only the arms were Roland's or his arms were like Roland's, hard and bulging and fast, and then sometimes his face became Roland's or Roland's his so he didn't know in his daydream whether he was watching Roland or Roland was watching him or whether he had become a stronger Paul or had become instead someone else.

'You talk about him a lot.'

'I don't think so.'

'Sometimes he's all you talk about.'

'Well, I like him. Come on; let's go to the fights.'

That night the gym was filled. Clusters of Paul's classmates were scattered through the crowd of men and women and students; Paul and Eddie sat in front of some girls they did not know. They were from the public high school and smelled of perfume and chewing gum. The lights went off except for the light over the ring and then Roland was climbing into it, stepping through the ropes held apart by the coach; Paul's gaze fixed on that. Paul was not close enough to see Roland's eyes but he knew from his profiled jaw and lips and his arms stretched to the ropes as he worked his feet in the rosin box that he was not afraid. Then the bell rang and Paul knew it was true: Roland glided into the ring and in purple trunks and gold sleeveless jersey he danced and jabbed and hooked and crossed, and within a minute the other boy was bewildered, lunging, swinging wildly, and backing up. The sounds of Roland's large stinging gloves filled the gym, grabbed yells from the throats of men and soft cries from the girls behind Paul. In the third round the other boy's nose suddenly bled; the red spurt covered his mouth and flowed onto his shirt while Roland closed in with a flurry and the referee pranced between them and stopped the fight. Roland put his arm around the boy's back, rested a glove on his shoulder, and walked him to the corner, toward his coach who was bringing a white towel.

Every Friday night he won and when the fights were at home Paul and Eddie watched. Eddie liked it too and walking home from the Saturday serial and cowboy movies he talked about Roland last night with the speed of a striking snake. Since his fight with Wayne,

Roland had moved among those boys who from the third grade had
been the athletes and class officers and good students as well and
who were growing into halfbacks and quarterbacks and fullbacks
and ends. Larry Guidry did not go into that world. He did not
seem to even look at it. Nor did they look at him. At the end of the
season Roland went to Baton Rouge and won the state cham-
pionship. When he came back to school, Paul waited for his chance,
got it between classes, and shook his hand.

On most days when the final bell rang and they had recited the
last decade of the rosary Paul got quickly out of the door and was
down the corridor and outside before Larry could hurt him. Sometimes as he fled Larry kicked his rump or punched his back. But
usually he escaped and rode home on his bicycle while Larry
waited in front of school for the bus. One April afternoon he and
Eddie walked across the front lawn of the school, Paul glancing at
the boys waiting for school buses; he did not see Larry; they walked
past the group and into town, to Borden's. When they got back to
school licking their ice-cream cones the buses had come and the
boys were gone and Larry was on the sidewalk, crouched beside his
bicycle, twisting a broken spoke around one that was intact. Paul
quickened his pace but Larry saw their legs and looked up. Then he
stood. Paul kept looking at the bicycle. It was green and had been
thickly repainted, by hand, and Paul thought of Larry with his
intent face and a paint brush, painting. The rear fender was dented.
    'Broken spoke?' Paul said.
    Larry watched him.
    'What's it doing, hitting the chain guard?'
    Larry reached out and took the ice-cream cone from Paul's hand.
It was chocolate, and Paul smiled and watched him taking a large
bite. Larry's tongue darted over the ice cream, licked it till it was a
smooth mound; he took another large bite and sucked it. Then he
licked again. He was getting close to the cone. When the ice cream
was level with the cone he bit into its rim, turning it and biting, and
then with one large bite he ate the small end. He had not looked at
Paul. He was turning to his bicycle when Eddie said: 'Well, I hope
you enjoyed your ice-cream cone.'

Larry had both hands on the handlebars and one foot poised at the kickstand; he spun quickly and with his right hand slapped the cone from Eddie's fist and then with the same hand a fist now he hit Eddie in the stomach and Eddie doubled over holding his stomach and gasping, but from his hurt and panicked face there was no sound. Paul knew where Larry had hit him; he had read about the body and its vulnerable spots and how he could use them, and he knew that Eddie now was not only in pain but he could not breathe. He watched Larry watching Eddie, watched the burning eyes. Eddie was shuffling in a semicircle. Still he did not make a sound. Then bent over he walked past Larry and onto the front lawn, toward the school, toward the back of it where his bicycle was. For a moment Paul watched him. Then smiling at Larry he went after Eddie and, from behind him, placed a hand on his shoulder.

'Eddie? Are you all right?'

Eddie shook his head. Looking down from Eddie's rear Paul saw the left cheek turning red. Then with a hoarse wheeze Eddie breathed. He breathed deeply and let it out fast and still bent forward he breathed again. He kept walking and Paul's hand dropped behind him. He stopped and breathed again and stood straight; Paul moved beside him and looked at his face and the tears on his cheeks.

'Are you okay?'

'I'm going home,' Eddie said; his shoulders jerking, he crossed the lawn toward the school. Paul watched him go. His back was to Larry. Then he shifted so he was profiled to Larry. When Eddie had gone around the corner of the school Paul looked at Larry, who leaned on his bicycle, watching.

'You sure got him,' Paul said. 'Right in the solar plexus.'

Larry moved his hands to the handlebars and kicked up the kickstand.

'You could probably beat Roland. Do you think you could beat Roland?'

There was neither fear nor challenge in Larry's eyes, only the dark watching, so quiet and removed that looking into Larry's eyes Paul seemed to be watching himself. They stood perhaps forty feet apart but Paul felt Larry's closeness, as though they were seated in school, with Larry at his back through the years, and he seemed to smell the starched khakis, the hair oil, the sweat, and the mustard and milk after lunch. Then Larry rode away.

That summer on a July afternoon Larry Guidry drowned in Black Bayou. The police found his bicycle and snowball cart on the bank, and beside them were his clothes and sneakers. That was the day after his parents told the police he had not come home. In the evening paper there were front-page photographs of policemen on the bank of the bayou, and men in outboards, dragging the muddy bottom. There was also a school picture of Larry; Paul remembered the day last fall when they had combed their hair and lined up to sit on the stool. He remembered he had hay fever that day and while the photographer took his picture he held his breath so he wouldn't sneeze. They found Larry at the bottom of the bayou. It was a hot afternoon and he had gone swimming alone.

'He was in your *class*?' Amy said at supper.

'He should never have gone in the bayou,' his mother said. 'It's treacherous.'

'Did you know him well?' Barbara said.

'I sat right in front of him for three years.'

That night he calmly prepared for sleep: kissed his father and mother and sisters and kneeled in prayer while inside the vast cavern of his body he shivered and tingled in anticipation of what waited for him in bed. He did not think Larry had committed any real mortal sins, with all the conditions they required, so he would not be in hell but in the fire of purgatory where souls thrashed in pain but their faces gazed with the serenity of hope; caressing his heart with a prayer he asked God to take Larry out of purgatory soon, and he saw him in khakis in the flames, his small hard hands clasped beneath his upturned housedust face. Then in bed Paul saw in the dark between him and the pale ceiling Larry getting off his bicycle and looking at the muddy bayou. For a while Larry stood looking at it; in the middle a stick swirled and went downstream. Then he undressed and walked down the bank and into the water. The bottom was soft and slippery and he threw himself forward in the shallow water and began to swim. Near the middle of the bayou the current hit him. He turned and stroked toward shallow water but the current pushed and twisted him, a thousand hands on his body, and in moaning panic he swallowed water and his arms weakened, his legs dragged heavily behind him, then he was under, somersaulting down and down, an acrobat slowly sinking in thick muddy water that rushed into his throat as he sank until he lay at the bottom, in the deep soft mud. He lay on his back, his arms angling out from his body, his mouth open and eyes closed, as in sleep. He lay in the dark cold all afternoon and all night and when the sun rose he was down there and he lay all morning until a grappling hook came slowly toward him in a cloud of mud like brown smoke.

Graduation

SOMETIMES, out in California, she wanted to tell her husband. That was after they had been married for more than two years (by then she was twenty-one) and she had settled into the familiarity so close to friendship but not exactly that either: she knew his sounds while he slept, brought some recognition to the very weight of his body next to her in bed, knew without looking the expressions on his face when he spoke. As their habits merged into common ritual, she began to feel she had never had another friend. Geography had something to do with this too. Waiting for him at the pier after the destroyer had been to sea for five days, or emerging from a San Diego movie theater, holding his hand, it seemed to her that the first eighteen years of her life in Port Arthur, Texas had no meaning at all. So, at times like that, she wanted to tell him.

She would look at the photograph which she had kept hidden for four years now, and think, as though she were speaking to him: *I was seventeen years old, a senior in high school, and I got up that day just like any other day and ate Puffed Wheat or something with my parents and went to school and there it was, on the bulletin board*—But she didn't tell him, for she knew that something was wrong: the photograph and her years in Port Arthur were true, and now her marriage in San Diego was true. But it seemed that for both of them to remain true they had to exist separately, one as history, one as now, and that if she disclosed the history, then those two truths added together would somehow produce a lie which in turn would call for more analysis than she cared to give. Or than she cared for her husband to give. So she would simply look at the picture of herself at sixteen, then put it away, in an old compact at the bottom of her jewelry box.

The picture had been cut out of the high school yearbook. Her blonde hair had been short then, an Italian boy; her face was tilted down and to one side, she was smiling at the camera, and beneath her face, across her sweater, was written: *Good piece.*

It had been thumbtacked to the bulletin board approximately two years after she had lost her virginity, parked someplace with a boy she loved. When they broke up she was still fifteen, a long way from marriage, and she wanted her virginity back. But this was impossible, for he had told all his friends. So she gave herself to the next boy whose pledge was a class ring or football sweater, and the one after that (before graduation night there were three of them, all with loose tongues) and everyone knew about Bobbie Huxford and she knew they did.

She never found out who put the picture on the bulletin board. When she got to school that day, a group of students were standing in the hall; they parted to let her through. Then she met the eyes of a girl, and saw neither mischief nor curiosity but fascination. A boy glanced at the bulletin board and quickly to the floor, and Bobbie saw the picture. She walked through them, pulled out the thumbtacks, forcing herself to go slowly, taking out each one and pressing it back into the board. She dropped the picture into her purse and went down the hall to her locker.

So at graduation she was not leaving the camaraderie, the perfunctory education, the ball games and dances and drives on a Sunday afternoon; she was leaving a place where she had always felt watched, except when Sherri King had been seduced by an uncle and somehow that word had got out. But the Kings had moved within a month, and Bobbie's classmates went back to watching her again. Still there was nostalgia: sitting on the stage, looking at the audience in the dark, she was remembering songs. Each of her loves had had a song, one she had danced to, pressed sweating and tight-gripped and swaying in dance halls where they served beer to anyone and the juke box never stopped: Nat 'King' Cole singing 'Somewhere Along the Way,' 'Trying' by the Hilltoppers, 'Your Cheatin' Heart' by Joni James, all of them plaintive songs: you drank two or three beers and clenched and dipped and weaved on the dance floor, and you squeezed him, your breasts against his firm narrow chest feeling like your brassiere and wrinkled blouse and his damp shirt weren't even there; you kept one hand on the back of his neck, sweat dripped between your fused cheeks, and you sang in nearly a whisper with Joni or Nat and you gave him a hard squeeze and said in his ear: *I love you, I'll love you forever.*

She had not loved any of them forever. With each one something had gone sour, but she was able to look past that, farther back to the good times. So there was that: sitting on the stage she remembered the songs, the love on waxed dance floors. But nostalgia wasn't the best part. She was happy, as she had been dancing to those songs that articulated her feelings and sent them flowing back into her blood, her heart. This time she didn't want to hold anyone, not even love anyone. She wanted to fly: soar away from everything, go higher than rain. She wanted to leave home, where bright and flowered drapes hung and sunlight moved through the day from one end of the maroon sofa to the other and formed motes in the air but found dustless the coffee table and the Bible that set on it.

She was their last child, an older brother with eight years in the Army and going for twenty, and an older sister married to a pharmacist in Beaumont, never having gone farther than Galveston in her whole life and bearing kids now like that was the only thing to do.

In the quiet summer afternoons when her mother was taking a nap and her father was at work, she felt both them and the immaculate house stifling her. One night returning from a date she had walked quietly into the kitchen. From there she could hear them snoring. Standing in the dark kitchen she smoked a cigarette, flicking the ashes in her hand (there was only one ash tray in the house and it was used by guests). Then looking at their bedroom door she suddenly wanted to holler: *I drank too much beer tonight and got sick in the john and Bud gave me 7-Up and creme de menthe to settle my stomach and clean my breath so I could still screw and that's what we did:* WE SCREWED. *That's what we always do.*

Now, looking out into the dark, Bobbie wondered if her parents were watching her. Then she knew they were, and they were proud. She was their last child, she was grown now, they had done their duty (college remained but they did not consider it essential) and now in the clean brightly-colored house they could wait with calm satisfaction for their souls to be wafted to heaven. Then she was sad. Because from the anxiety and pain of her birth until their own deaths, they had loved her and would love her without ever knowing who she was.

After the ceremony there was an all-night party at Rhonda Miller's camp. Bobbie's date was a tall shy boy named Calvin Tatman, who was popular with the boys but rarely dated; three days before graduation he had called Bobbie and asked her to be his date for Rhonda's party. The Millers' camp was on a lake front, surrounded by woods; behind the small house there was a large outdoor kitchen, screened on all sides. In the kitchen was a keg of beer, paper cups, and Rhonda's record player; that was how the party began. Several parents were there, drinking bourbon from the grown-ups' bar at one side of the kitchen; they got tight, beamed at the young people jitterbugging, and teased them about their sudden liking for cigarettes and beer. After a while Mr. Miller went outside to the barbecue pit and put on some hamburgers.

At first Bobbie felt kindly toward Calvin and thought since it was a big night, she would let him neck with her. But after Calvin had a few tall cups of beer she changed her mind. He stopped jitterbugging with her, dancing only the slow dances, holding her very close; then, a dance ended, he would join the boys at the keg. He didn't exactly leave her on the dance floor; she could follow him to the keg if she wanted to, and she did that a couple of times, then stopped. Once she watched him talking to the boys and she knew exactly what was going on: he had brought her because he couldn't get another date (she had already known that, absorbed it, spent a long time preparing her face and hair anyway), but now he was saving face by telling people he had brought her because he wanted to get laid.

Then other things happened. She was busy dancing, so she didn't notice for a while that she hadn't really had a conversation with anyone. She realized this when she left Calvin at the beer keg and joined the line outside at the barbecue pit, where Mr. Miller was serving hamburgers. She was last in line. She told Mr. Miller it was a wonderful party, then she went to the table beside the barbecue pit and made her hamburger. When she turned to go back to the kitchen, no one was waiting: two couples were just going in the door, and Bobbie was alone with Mr. Miller. She hesitated, telling herself that it meant nothing, that no one waited for people at barbecue pits. Still, if she went in alone, who would she sit with? She sat on the grass by the barbecue pit and talked to Mr. Miller. He ate a hamburger with her and gave her bourbon and water from the one-man bar he had set up to get him through the cooking. He was a stout, pleasant man, and he told her she was the best-looking girl at the party.

As soon as she entered the kitchen she knew people had been waiting for her. The music and talk were loud, but she also felt the silence of waiting; looking around, she caught a few girls watching her. Then, at her side, Rhonda said: 'Where you been, Bobbie?'

She glanced down at Rhonda, who sat with her boy friend, a class ring dangling from a chain around her neck, one possessive hand on Charlie Wright's knee. She doubted that Rhonda was a virgin but she had heard very little gossip because she had no girl friends. Now she went to the keg, pushed through the boys, and filled a cup.

Some time later, when the second keg had been tapped and both she and Calvin were drunk, he took her outside. She knew by now that everyone at the party was waiting to see if Calvin would make out. She went with him as far as the woods, kissed him standing up, worked her tongue in his mouth until he trembled and gasped; when he touched her breast she spun away and went back to the kitchen, jerking out of his grasp each time he clutched her arm. He was cursing her but she wasn't afraid. If he got rough, they were close enough to the kitchen so she could shout for Mr. Miller. Then Calvin was quiet anyway, realizing that if anyone heard they would know what had happened. When they stepped into the kitchen people were grinning at them. Bobbie went to the beer keg and Calvin danced with the first girl he saw.

When Charlie Wright got drunk he came over and danced with her. They swayed to 'Blue Velvet,' moved toward the door, and stumbled outside. They lay on the ground just inside the woods; because of the beer he took a long time and Bobbie thought of Rhonda waiting, faking a smile, dancing, waiting. . . Charlie told her she did it better than Rhonda. When they returned to the kitchen, Rhonda's face was pale; she did not dance with Charlie for the rest of the night.

At breakfast, near dawn, she sat on the bar and ate bacon and eggs with Mr. Miller, hoping Rhonda would worry about that too. Calvin tried to leave without her, but she had taken his car key, so he had to drive her home. It was just after sunrise, he was drunk, and he almost missed two curves.

'Hell, Calvin,' she said, 'just 'cause you can't make out doesn't mean you got to kill us.'

He swung at her, the back of his open hand striking her cheekbone, and all the way home she cried. Next day there was not even a bruise.

The lawnmower woke her that afternoon. She listened to it, knowing she had been hearing it for some time, had been fighting it in her sleep. Then she got up, took two aspirins which nearly gagged her, and made coffee and drank it in the kitchen, wanting a cigarette but still unable to tell her parents that she smoked. So she went outside and helped her father rake the grass. The day was hot; bent over the rake she sweated and fought with her stomach and shut her eyes to the pain pulsing in her head and she wished she had at least douched with a Coke, something she had heard about but had never done. Then she wished she had a Coke right now, with ice, and some more aspirin and a cool place in the house to sit very still. She did not want to marry Charlie Wright. Then she had to smile at herself, looking down at the grass piling under her rake. Charlie would not marry her. By this time everyone in school knew she had done it with him last night, and they probably thought she had done it with Calvin too. If she were pregnant, it would be a joke.

That night she told her parents she wanted to finish college as soon as possible so she could earn her own money. They agreed to send her to summer school at L.S.U., and two weeks later they drove her to Baton Rouge. During those two weeks she had seen no one; Charlie had called twice for dates, but she had politely turned him down, with excuses; she had menstruated, felt the missed life flowing as a new life for herself. Then she went away. Sitting in the back of the car, driving out of Port Arthur, she felt incomplete: she had not told anyone she was going to summer school, had not told anyone goodbye.

She went home after the summer term, then again at Thanksgiving, each time feeling more disengaged from her house and the town. When she went home for Christmas vacation, her father met her at the bus station. It was early evening. She saw him as the bus turned in: wiry, a little slumped, wearing the hat that wasn't a Stetson but looked like one. He spoke of the Christmas lights being ready and she tried to sound pleased. She even tried to feel pleased. She thought of him going to all that trouble every Christmas and maybe part of it was for her; maybe it had all started for her delight, long ago when she was a child. But when they reached the house she was again appalled by the lights strung on its front and the lighted manger her father had built years before and every Christmas placed on the lawn: a Nativity absurdly without animals or shepherds or wise men or even parents for the Child Jesus (a doll: Bobbie's) who lay utterly alone, wrapped in blankets on the straw floor of the manger. Holding her father's arm she went into the kitchen and hugged her mother, whose plumpness seemed emblematic of a woman who was kind and good and clean. Bobbie marvelled at the decorated house, then sat down to supper and talk of food and family news. After supper she told them, with even more nervousness than she had anticipated, that she had started smoking and she hoped they didn't mind. They both frowned, then her mother sighed and said:

'Well, I guess you're a big girl now.'

She was. For at L.S.U. she had learned this: you could become a virgin again. She finally understood that it was a man's word. They didn't mean you had done it once; they meant you did it, the lost hymen testimony not of the past but the present, and you carried with you a flavor of accessibility. She thought how much she would have been spared if she had known it at fifteen when she had felt changed forever, having focused on the word *loss* as though an arm or leg had been amputated, so she had given herself again, trying to be happy with her new self, rather than backing up and starting over, which would have been so easy because Willie Sorrells—her first lover—was not what you would call irresistible. Especially in retrospect.

But at L.S.U. she was a virgin; she had dated often in summer and fall, and no one had touched her. Not even Frank Mixon, whom she planned to marry, though he hadn't asked her yet. He was an economics major at Tulane, and a football player. He was also a senior. In June he was going into the Navy as an ensign and this was one of her reasons for wanting to marry him. And she had him fooled.

One night, though, she had scared herself. It was after the Tulane-L.S.U. game, the traditional game which Tulane traditionally lost. It was played in Baton Rouge. After the game Bobbie and Frank double-dated with the quarterback, Roy Lockhart, and his fiancee, Annie Broussard. Some time during the evening of bar-hopping, when they were all high, Roy identified a girl on the dance floor by calling her Jack Shelton's roommate of last year.

'What?' Bobbie said. 'What did you say?'

'Never mind,' Roy said.

'No: listen. Wait a minute.'

Then she started. All those things she had thought about and learned in silence came out, controlled, lucid, as though she had been saying them for years. At one point she realized Frank was watching her, quiet and rather awed, but a little suspiciously too. She kept talking, though.

'You fumbled against Vanderbilt,' she said to Roy. 'Should we call you fumbler for the rest of your life?'

Annie, the drunkest of the four, kept saying: That's *right*, that's *right*. Finally Bobbie said:

'Anyway, that's what *I* think.'

Frank put his arm around her.

'That takes care of gossip for tonight,' he said. 'Anybody want to talk about the game?'

'We tied 'em till the half,' Roy said. 'Then we should have gone home.'

'It wasn't your fault, fumbler,' Annie said, and she was still laughing when the others had stopped and ordered more drinks.

When Frank took Bobbie to the dormitory, they sat in the car, kissing. Then he said:

'You were sort of worked up tonight.'

'It happened to a friend of mine in high school. They ruined her. It's hard to believe, that you can ruin somebody with just talking, but they did it.'

He nodded, and moved to kiss her, but she pulled away.

'But that's not the only reason,' she said.

She shifted on the car seat and looked at his face, a good ruddy face, hair neither long nor short and combed dry, the college cut that would do for business as well; he was a tall strong young man, and because of his size and strength she felt that his gentleness was a protective quality reserved for her alone; but this wasn't true either, for she had never known him to be unkind to anyone and, even tonight, as he drank too much in post-game defeat, he only got quieter and sweeter.

'I don't have one either,' she said.

At first he did not understand. Then his face drew back and he looked out the windshield.

'It's not what you think. It's awful, and I'll never forget it but I've never told anyone, no one knows, they all think—'

Then she was crying into his coat, not at all surprised that her tears were real, and he was holding her.

'I was twelve years old,' she said.

She sat up, dried her cheeks, and looked away from him.

'It was an uncle, one of those uncles you never see. He was leaving someplace and going someplace else and he stopped off to see us for a couple of days. On the second night he came to my room and when I woke up he was doing it—'

'Hush,' he said. 'Hush, baby.'

She did not look at him.

'I was so scared, so awfully *scared*. So I didn't tell. Next morning I stayed in bed till he was gone. And I felt so rotten. Sometimes I still do, but not the way I did then. He's never come back to see us, but once in a while they mention him and I feel sick all over again, and I think about telling them but it's too late now, even if they did something to him it's too late, I can never get it back—'

For a long time that night Frank Mixon held his soiled girl in his arms, and, to Bobbie, those arms seemed quite strong, quite capable. She knew that she would marry him.

Less than a month later she was home for Christmas, untouched, changed. She spent New Year's at Frank's house in New Orleans. In the cold dusk after the Sugar Bowl game they walked back to his house to get the car and go to a party. Holding his arm, she watched a trolley go by, looked through car windows at attractive people leaving the stadium, breathed the smell of exhaust which was somehow pleasing, and the damp winter air, and another smell as of something old, as though from the old lives of the houses they passed. She knew that if she lived in New Orleans only a few months, Port Arthur would slide away into the Gulf. Climbing a gentle slope to his house, she was very tired, out of breath. The house was dark. Frank turned on a light and asked if she wanted a drink.

'God, no,' she said. 'I'd like to lie down for a few minutes.'

'Why don't you? I'll make some coffee.'

She climbed the stairs, turned on the hall light, and went to the guest room. She took off her shoes, lay clothed on the bed, and was asleep. His voice woke her: he stood at the bed, blocking the light from the hall. She propped on an elbow to drink the coffee, and asked him how long she had been asleep.

'About an hour.'

'What did you do?'

'Watched some of the Rose Bowl.'

'That was sweet. I'll hurry and get freshened up so we won't be too late.'

But when she set the empty cup on the bedside table he kissed her; then he was lying on top of her.

'Your folks—'

'They're at a party.'

She was yielding very slowly, holding him off tenderly then murmuring when his hand slipped into her blouse, stayed there, then withdrew to work on the buttons. She delayed, gave in, then stalled so that it took a long while for him to take off the blouse and brassiere. Finally they were naked, under the covers, and her hands on his body were shy. Then she spoke his name. With his first penetration she stiffened and he said It's all right, sweet darling Bobbie, it's all right now—and she eased forward, wanting to enfold him with her legs but she kept them outstretched, knees bent, and gave only tentative motion to her hips. When he was finished she held him there, his lips at her ear; she moved slowly as he whispered; then whimpering, shuddering, and concealing, she came.

'Will you?' he said. 'Will you marry me this June?'

'Oh *yes*,' she said, and squeezed his ribs. 'Yes I will. This is my first time and that other never happened, not ever, it's all over now—Oh I'm so *happy*, Frank, I'm so *happy*—'

The Fat Girl

ER NAME was Louise. Once when she was sixteen a boy kissed her at a barbecue; he was drunk and he jammed his tongue into her mouth and ran his hands up and down her hips. Her father kissed her often. He was thin and kind and she could see in his eyes when he looked at her the lights of love and pity.

It started when Louise was nine. You must start watching what you eat, her mother would say. I can see you have my metabolism. Louise also had her mother's pale blonde hair. Her mother was slim and pretty, carried herself erectly, and ate very little. The two of them would eat bare lunches, while her older brother ate sandwiches and potato chips, and then her mother would sit smoking while Louise eyed the bread box, the pantry, the refrigerator. Wasn't that good, her mother would say. In five years you'll be in high school and if you're fat the boys won't like you; they won't ask you out. Boys were as far away as five years, and she would go to her room and wait for nearly an hour until she knew her mother was no longer thinking of her, then she would creep into the kitchen and, listening to her mother talking on the phone, or her footsteps upstairs, she would open the bread box, the pantry, the jar of peanut butter. She would put the sandwich under her shirt and go outside or to the bathroom to eat it.

Her father was a lawyer and made a lot of money and came home looking pale and happy. Martinis put color back in his face, and at dinner he talked to his wife and two children. Oh give her a potato, he would say to Louise's mother. She's a growing girl. Her mother's voice then became tense: If she has a potato she shouldn't have dessert. She should have both, her father would say, and he would reach over and touch Louise's cheek or hand or arm.

In high school she had two girl friends and at night and on week-ends they rode in a car or went to movies. In movies she was fascinated by fat actresses. She wondered why they were fat. She knew why she was fat: she was fat because she was Louise. Because God had made her that way. Because she wasn't like her friends Joan and Marjorie, who drank milk shakes after school and were all bones and tight skin. But what about those actresses, with their talents, with their broad and profound faces? Did they eat as heedlessly as Bishop Humphries and his wife who sometimes came to dinner and, as Louise's mother said, gorged between amenities? Or did they try to lose weight, did they go about hungry and angry and thinking of food? She thought of them eating lean meats and salads with friends, and then going home and building strange large sandwiches with French bread. But mostly she believed they did not go through these failures; they were fat because they chose to be. And she was certain of something else too: she could see it in their faces: they did not eat secretly. Which she did: her creeping to the kitchen when she was nine became, in high school, a ritual of deceit and pleasure. She was a furtive eater of sweets. Even her two friends did not know her secret.

Joan was thin, gangling, and flat-chested; she was attractive enough and all she needed was someone to take a second look at her face, but the school was large and there were pretty girls in every classroom and walking all the corridors, so no one ever needed to take a second look at Joan. Marjorie was thin too, an intense, heavy-smoking girl with brittle laughter. She was very intelligent, and with boys she was shy because she knew she made them uncomfortable, and because she was smarter than they were and so could not understand or could not believe the levels they lived on. She was to have a nervous breakdown before earning her PhD. in philosophy at the University of California, where she met and married a physicist and discovered within herself an untrammelled passion: she made love with her husband on the couch, the carpet, in the bathtub, and on the washing machine. By that time much had happened to her and she never thought of Louise. Joan would finally stop growing and begin moving with grace and confidence. In college she would have two lovers and then several more during the six years she spent in Boston before marrying a middle-aged editor who had two sons in their early teens, who drank too much, who was tenderly, boyishly grateful for her love, and whose wife had been killed while rock-climbing in New Hampshire with her lover. She would not think of Louise either, except in an earlier time, when lovers were still new to her and she was ecstatically surprised each time one of them loved her and, sometimes at night, lying in a man's arms, she would tell how in high school no one dated her, she had been thin and plain (she would still believe that: that she had been plain; it had never been true) and so had been forced into the week-end and night-time company of a neurotic smart girl and a shy fat girl. She would say this with self-pity exaggerated by Scotch and her need to be more deeply loved by the man who held her.

She never eats, Joan and Marjorie said of Louise. They ate lunch with her at school, watched her refusing potatoes, ravioli, fried fish. Sometimes she got through the cafeteria line with only a salad. That is how they would remember her: a girl whose hapless body was destined to be fat. No one saw the sandwiches she made and took to her room when she came home from school. No one saw the store of Milky Ways, Butterfingers, Almond Joys, and Hersheys far back on her closet shelf, behind the stuffed animals of her childhood. She was not a hypocrite. When she was out of the house she truly believed she was dieting; she forgot about the candy, as a man speaking into his office dictaphone may forget the lewd photographs hidden in an old shoe in his closet. At other times, away from home, she thought of the waiting candy with near lust. One night driving home from a movie, Marjorie said: 'You're lucky you don't smoke; it's *incred*ible what I go through to hide it from my parents.' Louise turned to her a smile which was elusive and mysterious; she yearned to be home in bed, eating chocolate in the dark. She did not need to smoke; she already had a vice that was insular and destructive.

SHE BROUGHT it with her to college. She thought she would leave it behind. A move from one place to another, a new room without the haunted closet shelf, would do for her what she could not do for herself. She packed her large dresses and went. For two weeks she was busy with registration, with shyness, with classes;

then she began to feel at home. Her room was no longer like a motel. Its walls had stopped watching her, she felt they were her friends, and she gave them her secret. Away from her mother, she did not have to be as elaborate; she kept the candy in her drawer now.

The school was in Massachusetts, a girls' school. When she chose it, when she and her father and mother talked about it in the evenings, everyone so carefully avoided the word boys that sometimes the conversations seemed to be about nothing but boys. There are no boys there, the neuter words said; you will not have to contend with that. In her father's eyes were pity and encouragement; in her mother's was disappointment, and her voice was crisp. They spoke of courses, of small classes where Louise would get more attention. She imagined herself in those small classes; she saw herself as a teacher would see her, as the other girls would; she would get no attention.

The girls at the school were from wealthy families, but most of them wore the uniform of another class: blue jeans and work shirts, and many wore overalls. Louise bought some overalls, washed them until the dark blue faded, and wore them to classes. In the cafeteria she ate as she had in high school, not to lose weight nor even to sustain her lie, but because eating lightly in public had become as habitual as good manners. Everyone had to take gym, and in the locker room with the other girls, and wearing shorts on the volleyball and badminton courts, she hated her body. She liked her body most when she was unaware of it: in bed at night, as sleep gently took her out of her day, out of herself. And she liked parts of her body. She liked her brown eyes and sometimes looked at them in the mirror: they were not shallow eyes, she thought; they were indeed windows of a tender soul, a good heart. She liked her lips and nose, and her chin, finely shaped between her wide and sagging cheeks. Most of all she liked her long pale blonde hair, she liked washing and drying it and lying naked on her bed, smelling of shampoo, and feeling the soft hair at her neck and shoulders and back.

Her friend at college was Carrie, who was thin and wore thick glasses and often at night she cried in Louise's room. She did not know why she was crying. She was crying, she said, because she was unhappy. She could say no more. Louise said she was unhappy too, and Carrie moved in with her. One night Carrie talked for hours, sadly and bitterly, about her parents and what they did to each other. When she finished she hugged Louise and they went to bed. Then in the dark Carrie spoke across the room: 'Louise? I just wanted to tell you. One night last week I woke up and smelled chocolate. You were eating chocolate, in your bed. I wish you'd eat it in front of me, Louise, whenever you feel like it.'

Stiffened in her bed, Louise could think of nothing to say. In the silence she was afraid Carrie would think she was asleep and would tell her again in the morning or tomorrow night. Finally she said Okay. Then after a moment she told Carrie if she ever wanted any she could feel free to help herself; the candy was in the top drawer. Then she said thank you.

They were roommates for four years and in the summers they exchanged letters. Each fall they greeted with embraces, laughter, tears, and moved into their old room, which had been stripped and cleansed of them for the summer. Neither girl enjoyed summer. Carrie did not like being at home because her parents did not love each other. Louise lived in a small city in Louisiana. She did not like summer because she had lost touch with Joan and Marjorie; they saw each other, but it was not the same. She liked being with her father but with no one else. The flicker of disappointment in her mother's eyes at the airport was a vanguard of the army of relatives and acquaintances who awaited her: they would see her on the streets, in stores, at the country club, in her home, and in theirs; in the first moments of greeting, their eyes would tell her she was still fat Louise, who had been fat as long as they could remember, who had gone to college and returned as fat as ever. Then their eyes dismissed her, and she longed for school and Carrie, and she wrote letters to her friend. But that saddened her too. It wasn't simply that Carrie was her only friend, and when they finished college they might never see each other again. It was that her existence in the world was so divided; it had begun when she was a child creeping to the kitchen; now that division was much sharper, and her friendship with Carrie seemed disproportionate and perilous. The world she was destined to live in had nothing to do with the intimate nights in their room at school.

In the summer before their senior year, Carrie fell in love. She wrote to Louise about him, but she did not write much, and this hurt Louise more than if Carrie had shown the joy her writing tried to conceal. That fall they returned to their room; they were still close and warm, Carrie still needed Louise's ears and heart at night as she spoke of her parents and her recurring malaise whose source the two friends never discovered. But on most week-ends Carrie left, and caught a bus to Boston where her boy friend studied music. During the week she often spoke hesitantly of sex; she was not sure if she liked it. But Louise, eating candy and listening, did not know whether Carrie was telling the truth or whether, as in her letters of the past summer, Carrie was keeping from her those delights she may never experience.

Then one Sunday night when Carrie had just returned from Boston and was unpacking her overnight bag, she looked at Louise and said: 'I was thinking about you. On the bus coming home tonight.' Looking at Carrie's concerned, determined face, Louise prepared herself for humiliation. 'I was thinking about when we graduate. What you're going to do. What's to become of you. I want you to be loved the way I love you. Louise, if I help you, *real*ly help you, will you go on a diet?'

LOUISE ENTERED a period of her life she would remember always, the way some people remember having endured poverty. Her diet did not begin the next day. Carrie told her to eat on Monday as though it were the last day of her life. So for the first time since grammar school Louise went into a school cafeteria and ate everything she wanted. At breakfast and lunch and dinner she glanced around the table to see if the other girls noticed the food on her tray. They did not. She felt there was a lesson in this, but it lay beyond her grasp. That night in their room she ate the four remaining candy bars. During the day Carrie rented a small refrigerator, bought an electric skillet, an electric broiler, and bathroom scales.

On Tuesday morning Louise stood on the scales, and Carrie wrote in her notebook: *October 14: 184 lbs.* Then she made Louise a cup of black coffee and scrambled one egg and sat with her while she ate. When Carrie went to the dining room for breakfast, Louise walked about the campus for thirty minutes. That was part of the plan. The campus was pretty, on its lawns grew at least one of every tree native to New England, and in the warm morning sun Louise felt a new hope. At noon they met in their room, and Carrie broiled her a piece of hamburger and served it with lettuce. Then while Carrie ate in the dining room Louise walked again. She was weak with hunger and she felt queasy. During her afternoon classes she was nervous and tense, and she chewed her pencil and tapped her heels on the floor and tightened her calves. When she returned to her room late that afternoon, she was so glad to see Carrie that she embraced her; she had felt she could not bear another minute of hunger, but now with Carrie she knew she could make it at least through tonight. Then she would sleep and face tomorrow when it came. Carrie broiled her a steak and served it with lettuce. Louise studied while Carrie ate dinner, then they went for a walk.

That was her ritual and her diet for the rest of the year, Carrie alternating fish and chicken breasts with the steaks for dinner, and every day was nearly as bad as the first. In the evenings she was irritable. In all her life she had never been afflicted by ill temper and she looked upon it now as a demon which, along with hunger, was taking possession of her soul. Often she spoke sharply to Carrie. One night during their after-dinner walk Carrie talked sadly of night, of how darkness made her more aware of herself, and at night she did not know why she was in college, why she studied, why she was walking the earth with other people. They were standing on a wooden foot bridge, looking down at a dark pond. Carrie kept talking; perhaps soon she would cry. Suddenly Louise said: 'I'm sick of lettuce. I never want to see a piece of lettuce for the rest of my life. I hate it. We shouldn't even buy it, it's immoral.'

Carrie was quiet. Louise glanced at her, and the pain and irritation in Carrie's face soothed her. Then she was ashamed. Before she could say she was sorry, Carrie turned to her and said gently: 'I know. I know how terrible it is.'

Carrie did all the shopping, telling Louise she knew how hard it was to go into a supermarket when you were hungry. And Louise was always hungry. She drank diet soft drinks and started smoking Carrie's cigarettes, learned to enjoy inhaling, thought of cancer and emphysema but they were as far away as those boys her mother had talked about when she was nine. By Thanksgiving she was smoking over a pack a day and her weight in Carrie's notebook was one hundred and sixty-two pounds. Carrie was afraid if Louise went home at Thanksgiving she would lapse from the diet, so Louise spent the vacation with Carrie, in Philadelphia. Carrie wrote her family about the diet, and told Louise that she had. On the plane to Philadelphia, Louise said: 'I feel like a bedwetter. When I was a little girl I had a friend who used to come spend the night and Mother would put a rubber sheet on the bed and we all pretended there wasn't a rubber sheet and that she hadn't wet the bed. Even me, and I slept with her.' At Thanksgiving dinner she lowered her eyes as Carrie's father put two slices of white meat on her plate and passed it to her over the bowls of steaming food.

When she went home at Christmas she weighed a hundred and fifty-five pounds; at the airport her mother marvelled. Her father laughed and hugged her and said: 'But now there's less of you to love.' He was troubled by her smoking but only mentioned it once; he told her she was beautiful and, as always, his eyes bathed her with love. During the long vacation her mother cooked for her as Carrie had, and Louise returned to school weighing a hundred and forty-six pounds.

Flying north on the plane she warmly recalled the surprised and congratulatory eyes of her relatives and acquaintances. She had not seen Joan or Marjorie. She thought of returning home in May, weighing the hundred and fifteen pounds which Carrie had in October set as their goal. Looking toward the stoic days ahead, she felt strong. She thought of those hungry days of fall and early winter (and now: she was hungry now: with almost a frown, almost a brusque shake of the head, she refused peanuts from the stewardess): those first weeks of the diet when she was the pawn of an irascibility which still, conditioned to her ritual as she was, could at any moment take command of her. She thought of the nights of trying to sleep while her stomach growled. She thought of her addiction to cigarettes. She thought of the people at school: not one teacher, not one girl, had spoken to her about her loss of weight, not even about her absence from meals. And without warning her spirit collapsed. She did not feel strong, she did not feel she was committed to and within reach of achieving a valuable goal. She felt that somehow she had lost more than pounds of fat; that some time during her dieting she had lost herself too. She tried to remember what it had felt like to be Louise before she had started living on meat and fish, as an unhappy adult may look sadly in the memory of childhood for lost virtues and hopes. She looked down at the earth far below, and it seemed to her that her soul, like her body aboard the plane, was in some rootless flight. She neither knew its destination nor where it had departed from; it was on some passage she could not even define.

During the next few weeks she lost weight more slowly and once for eight days Carrie's daily recording stayed at a hundred and thirty-six. Louise woke in the morning thinking of one hundred and thirty-six and then she stood on the scales and they echoed her. She became obsessed with that number, and there wasn't a day when she didn't say it aloud, and through the days and nights the number stayed in her mind, and if a teacher had spoken those digits in a classroom she would have opened her mouth to speak. What if that's me, she said to Carrie. I mean what if a hundred and thirty-six is my real weight and I just can't lose anymore. Walking hand-in-hand with her despair was a longing for this to be true, and that longing angered her and wearied her, and every day she was gloomy. On the ninth day she weighed a hundred and thirty-five and a half pounds. She was not relieved; she thought bitterly of the months ahead, the shedding of the last twenty and a half pounds.

On Easter Sunday, which she spent at Carrie's, she weighed one hundred and twenty pounds, and she ate one slice of glazed pineapple with her ham and lettuce. She did not enjoy it: she felt she was being friendly with a recalcitrant enemy who had once tried to destroy her. Carrie's parents were laudative. She liked them and she wished they would touch sometimes, and look at each other when they spoke. She guessed they would divorce when Carrie left home, and she vowed that her own marriage would be one of affection and tenderness. She could think about that now: marriage. At school she had read in a Boston paper that this summer the cicadas would come out of their seventeen year hibernation on Cape Cod, for a month they would mate and then die, leaving their young to burrow into the ground where they would stay for seventeen years. That's me, she had said to Carrie. Only my hibernation lasted twenty-one years.

Often her mother asked in letters and on the phone about the diet, but Louise answered vaguely. When she flew home in late May she weighed a hundred and thirteen pounds, and at the airport her mother cried and hugged her and said again and again: You're so *beaut*iful. Her father blushed and bought her a martini. For days her relatives and acquaintances congratulated her, and the applause in their eyes lasted the entire summer, and she loved their eyes, and swam in the country club pool, the first time she had done this since she was a child.

S HE LIVED at home and ate the way her mother did and every morning she weighed herself on the scales in her bathroom. Her mother liked to take her shopping and buy her dresses and they put her old ones in the Goodwill box at the shopping center; Louise thought of them existing on the body of a poor woman whose cheap meals kept her fat. Louise's mother had a photographer come to the house, and Louise posed on the couch and standing beneath a live oak and sitting in a wicker lawn chair next to an azalea bush. The new clothes and the photographer made her feel she was going to another country or becoming a citizen of a new one. In the fall she took a job of no consequence, to give herself something to do.

Also in the fall a young lawyer joined her father's firm, he came one night to dinner, and they started seeing each other. He was the first man outside her family to kiss her since the barbecue when she was sixteen. Louise celebrated Thanksgiving not with rice dressing and candied sweet potatoes and mince meat and pumpkin pies, but by giving Richard her virginity which she realized, at the very last moment of its existence, she had embarked on giving him over thirteen months ago, on that Tuesday in October when Carrie had made her a cup of black coffee and scrambled one egg. She wrote this to Carrie, who replied happily by return mail. She also, through glance and smile and innuendo, tried to tell her mother too. But finally she controlled that impulse, because Richard felt guilty about making love with the daughter of his partner and friend. In the spring they married. The wedding was a large one, in the Episcopal church, and Carrie flew from Boston to be maid of honor. Her parents had recently separated and she was living with the musician and was still victim of her unpredictable malaise. It overcame her on the night before the wedding, so Louise was up with her until past three and woke next morning from a sleep so heavy that she did not want to leave it.

Richard was a lean, tall, energetic man with the metabolism of a pencil sharpener. Louise fed him everything he wanted. He liked Italian food and she got recipes from her mother and watched him eating spaghetti with the sauce she had only tasted, and ravioli and lasagna, while she ate antipasto with her chianti. He made a lot of money and borrowed more and they bought a house whose lawn sloped down to the shore of a lake; they had a wharf and a boathouse, and Richard bought a boat and they took friends waterskiing. Richard bought her a car and they spent his vacations in Mexico, Canada, the Bahamas, and in the fifth year of their marriage they went to Europe and, according to their plan, she conceived a child in Paris. On the plane back, as she looked out the window and beyond the sparkling sea and saw her country, she felt that it was waiting for her, as her home by the lake was, and her parents, and her good friends who rode in the boat and waterskied; she thought of the accumulated warmth and pelf of her marriage, and how by slimming her body she had bought into the pleasures of the nation. She felt cunning, and she smiled to herself, and took Richard's hand.

But these moments of triumph were sparse. On most days she went about her routine of leisure with a sense of certainty about herself that came merely from not thinking. But there were times, with her friends, or with Richard, or alone in the house, when she was suddenly assaulted by the feeling that she had taken the wrong train and arrived at a place where no one knew her, and where she ought not to be. Often, in bed with Richard, she talked of being fat: 'I was the one who started the friendship with Carrie, I chose her, I started the conversations. When I understood that she was my friend I understood something else: I had chosen her for the same reason I'd chosen Joan and Marjorie. They were all thin. I was always thinking about what people saw when they looked at me and I didn't want them to see two fat girls. When I was alone I didn't mind being fat but then I'd have to leave the house again and then I didn't want to look like me. But at home I didn't mind except when I was getting dressed to go out of the house and when Mother looked at me. But I stopped looking at her when she looked at me. And in college I felt good with Carrie; there weren't any boys and I didn't have any other friends and so when I wasn't with Carrie I thought about her and I tried to ignore the other people around me, I tried to make them not exist. A lot of the time I could do that. It was strange, and I felt like a spy.'

If Richard was bored by her repetition he pretended not to be. But she knew the story meant very little to him. She could have been telling him of a childhood illness, or wearing braces, or a broken heart at sixteen. He could not see her as she was when she was fat. She felt as though she were trying to tell a foreign lover about her life in the United States, and if only she could command the language he would know and love all of her and she would feel complete. Some of the acquaintances of her childhood were her friends now, and even they did not seem to remember her when she was fat.

Now her body was growing again, and when she put on a maternity dress for the first time she shivered with fear. Richard did not smoke and he asked her, in a voice just short of demand, to stop during her pregnancy. She did. She ate carrots and celery instead of smoking, and at cocktail parties she tried to eat nothing, but after her first drink she ate nuts and cheese and crackers and dips. Always at these parties Richard had talked with his friends and she had rarely spoken to him until they drove home. But now when he noticed her at the hors d'oeuvres table he crossed the room and, smiling, led her back to his group. His smile and his hand on her arm told her he was doing his clumsy, husbandly best to help her through a time of female mystery.

She was gaining weight but she told herself it was only the baby, and would leave with its birth. But at other times she knew quite clearly that she was losing the discipline she had fought so hard to gain during her last year with Carrie. She was hungry now as she had been in college, and she ate between meals and after dinner and tried to eat only carrots and celery, but she grew to hate them, and her desire for sweets was as vicious as it had been long ago. At home she ate bread and jam and when she shopped for groceries she bought a candy bar and ate it driving home and put the wrapper in her purse and then in the garbage can under the sink. Her cheeks had filled out, there was loose flesh under her chin, her arms and legs were plump, and her mother was concerned. So was Richard. One night when she brought pie and milk to the living room where they were watching television, he said: 'You already had a piece. At dinner.'

She did not look at him.

'You're gaining weight. It's not all water, either. It's fat. It'll be summertime. You'll want to get into your bathing suit.'

The pie was cherry. She looked at it as her fork cut through it; she speared the piece and rubbed it in the red juice on the plate before lifting it to her mouth.

'You never used to eat pie,' he said. 'I just think you ought to watch it a bit. It's going to be tough on you this summer.'

In her seventh month, with a delight reminiscent of climbing the stairs to Richard's apartment before they were married, she returned to her world of secret gratification. She began hiding candy in her underwear drawer. She ate it during the day and at night while Richard slept, and at breakfast she was distracted, waiting for him to leave.

She gave birth to a son, brought him home, and nursed both him and her appetites. During this time of celibacy she enjoyed her body through her son's mouth; while he suckled she stroked his small head and back. She was hiding candy but she did not conceal her other indulgences: she was smoking again but still she ate between meals, and at dinner she ate what Richard did, and coldly he watched her, he grew petulant, and when the date marking the end of their celibacy came they let it pass. Often in the afternoons her mother visited and scolded her and Louise sat looking at the baby and said nothing until finally, to end it, she promised to diet. When her mother and father came for dinners, her father kissed her and held the baby and her mother said nothing about Louise's body, and her voice was tense. Returning from work in the evenings Richard looked at a soiled plate and glass on the table beside her chair as if detecting traces of infidelity, and at every dinner they fought.

'Look at you,' he said. 'Lasagna, for God's sake. When are you going to start? It's not simply that you haven't lost any weight. You're gaining. I can see it. I can feel it when you get in bed. Pretty soon you'll weigh more than I do and I'll be sleeping on a trampoline.'

'You never touch me anymore.'

'I don't want to touch you. Why should I? Have you *looked* at yourself?'

'You're cruel,' she said. 'I never knew how cruel you were.'

She ate, watching him. He did not look at her. Glaring at his plate, he worked with fork and knife like a hurried man at a lunch counter.

'I bet you didn't either,' she said.

That night when he was asleep she took a Milky Way to the bathroom. For a while she stood eating in the dark, then she turned on the light. Chewing, she looked at herself in the mirror; she looked at her eyes and hair. Then she stood on the scales and looking at the numbers between her feet, one hundred and sixty-two, she remembered when she had weighed a hundred and thirty-six pounds for eight days. Her memory of those eight days was fond and amusing, as though she were recalling an Easter egg hunt when she was six. She stepped off the scales and pushed them under the lavatory and did not stand on them again.

It was summer and she bought loose dresses and when Richard took friends out on the boat she did not wear a bathing suit or shorts; her friends gave her mischievous glances, and Richard did not look at her. She stopped riding on the boat. She told them she wanted to stay with the baby, and she sat inside holding him until she heard the boat leave the wharf. Then she took him to the front lawn and walked with him in the shade of the trees and talked to him about the blue jays and mockingbirds and cardinals she saw on their branches. Sometimes she stopped and watched the boat out on the lake and the friend skiing behind it.

Every day Richard quarrelled, and because his rage went no further than her weight and shape, she felt excluded from it, and she remained calm within layers of flesh and spirit, and watched his frustration, his impotence. He truly believed they were arguing about her weight. She knew better: she knew that beneath the argument lay the question of who Richard was. She thought of him smiling at the wheel of his boat, and long ago courting his slender girl, the daughter of his partner and friend. She thought of Carrie telling her of smelling chocolate in the dark and, after that, watching her eat it night after night. She smiled at Richard, teasing his anger.

H E IS ANGRY now. He stands in the center of the living room, raging at her, and he wakes the baby. Beneath Richard's voice she hears the soft crying, feels it in her heart, and quietly she rises from her chair and goes upstairs to the child's room and takes him from the crib. She brings him to the living room and sits holding him in her lap, pressing him gently against the folds of fat at her waist. Now Richard is pleading with her. Louise thinks tenderly of Carrie broiling meat and fish in their room, and walking with her in the evenings. She wonders if Carrie still has the malaise. Perhaps she will come for a visit. In Louise's arms now the boy sleeps.

'I'll help you,' Richard says. 'I'll eat the same things you eat.'

But his face does not approach the compassion and determination and love she had seen in Carrie's during what she now recognizes as the worst year of her life. She can remember nothing about that year except hunger, and the meals in her room. She is hungry now. When she puts the boy to bed she will get a candy bar from her room. She will eat it here, in front of Richard. This room will be hers soon. She considers the possibilities: all these rooms and the lawn where she can do whatever she wishes. She knows he will leave soon. It has been in his eyes all summer. She stands, using one hand to pull herself out of the chair. She carries the boy to his crib, feels him against her large breasts, feels that his sleeping body touches her soul. With a surge of vindication and relief she holds him. Then she kisses his forehead and places him in the crib. She goes to the bedroom and in the dark takes a bar of candy from her drawer. Slowly she descends the stairs. She knows Richard is waiting but she feels his departure so happily that, when she enters the living room, unwrapping the candy, she is surprised to see him standing there.

PART TWO

Cadence

to Tommie

HE STOOD in the summer Virginia twilight, an officer candidate, nineteen years old, wearing Marine utilities and helmet, an M1 rifle in one hand, its butt resting on the earth, a pack high on his back, the straps buckled too tightly around his shoulders; because he was short he was the last man in the rank. He stood in the front rank and watched Gunnery Sergeant Hathaway and Lieutenant Swenson in front of the platoon, talking quietly to each other, the lieutenant tall and confident, the sergeant short, squat, with a beer gut; at night, he had told them, he went home and drank beer with his old lady. He could walk the entire platoon into the ground. Or so he made them believe. He had small, brown, murderous eyes; he scowled when he was quiet or thinking; and, at rest, his narrow lips tended downward at the corners. Now he turned from the lieutenant and faced the platoon. They stood on the crest of a low hill; beyond Hathaway the earth sloped down to a darkened meadow and then rose again, a wooded hill whose black trees touched the grey sky.

'We're going back over the Hill Trail,' he said, and someone groaned and at first Paul fixed on that sound as a source of strength: someone else dreaded the hills as much as he did. Around him he could sense a fearful gathering of resolve, and now the groan he had first clung to became something else: a harbinger of his own failure. He knew that, except for Hugh Munson standing beside him, he was the least durable of all; and since these men, a good half of them varsity athletes, were afraid, his own fear became nearly unbearable. It became physical: it took a penetrating fall into his legs and weakened his knees so he felt he was not supported by muscle and bone but by faint nerves alone.

'We'll put the little men up front,' Hathaway said, 'so you long-legged pacesetters'll know what it's like to bring up the rear.'

They moved in two files, down a sloping trail flanked by black trees. Hugh was directly behind him. To his left, leading the other file, was Whalen; he was also short, five-eight or five-seven; but he was wide as a door. He was a wrestler from Purdue. They moved down past trees and thick underbrush into the dark of the woods, and behind him he heard the sounds of blindness: a thumping body and clattering rifle as someone tripped and fell; there were curses, and voices warned those coming behind them, told of a branch reaching across the trail; from the rear Hathaway called: 'Close it up close it up, don't lose sight of the man in front of you.' Paul walked step for step beside Whalen and watched tall Lieutenant Swenson setting the pace, watched his pack and helmet as he started to climb and, looking up and past the lieutenant, up the wide corridor between the trees, he saw against the sky the crest of the first hill.

Then he was climbing, his legs and lungs already screaming at him that they could not, and he saw himself at home in his room last winter and spring, getting ready for this: push-ups and sit-ups, leg lifts and squat jumps and deep kneebends, exercises which made his body feel good but did little for it, and as he climbed and the muscles of his thighs bulged and tightened and his lungs demanded more and more of the humid air, he despised that memory of himself, despised himself for being so far removed from the world of men that he had believed in calisthenics, had not even considered running, though he had six months to get in condition after signing the contract with the Marine captain who had come one day like salvation into the student union, wearing the blue uniform and the manly beauty that would fulfill Paul's dreams. Now those dreams were an illusion: he was close to the top of the first hill, his calf and thigh muscles burning, his lungs gasping, and his face, near sobbing, was fixed in pain. His one desire that he felt with each breath, each step up the hard face of the hill, was not endurance: it was deliverance. He wanted to go home, and to have this done for him in some magical or lucky way that would give him honor in his father's eyes. So as he moved over the top of the hill, Whalen panting beside him, and followed Lieutenant Swenson steeply down, he wished and then prayed that he would break his leg.

He descended: away from the moonlight, down into the shadows and toward the black at the foot of the hill. His strides were short now and quick, his body leaned backward so he wouldn't fall, and once again his instincts and his wishes were at odds: wanting a broken leg, he did not want to fall and break it; wanting to go home, he did not want to quit and pack his seabag and suitcase, and go. For there was that too: they would let him quit. That was the provision which had seemed harmless enough, even congenial, as he lifted his pen in the student union. He could stop and sit or lean against a tree and wait for the platoon to pass and Sergeant Hathaway's bulk to appear like an apparition of fortitude and conscience out of the dark, strong and harsh and hoarse, and he could then say: 'Sir, I want to go home.' It would be over then, he would drift onto the train tomorrow and then to the airport and fly home in a nimbus of shame to face his father's blue and humiliated eyes, which he had last seen beaming at him before the embrace that, four and a half weeks ago, sent him crossing the asphalt to the plane.

It was a Sunday. Sergeants met the planes in Washington and put the men on buses that were green and waxed, and drove them through the last of the warm setting sun to Quantico. The conversations aboard the bus were apprehensive and friendly. They all wore civilian clothes except Paul. At home he had joined the reserve and his captain had told him to wear his uniform and he had: starched cotton khaki, and it was wrinkled from his flight. The sergeants did not look at the uniform or at him either; or, if they did, they had a way of looking that was not looking at him. By the time he reached the barracks he felt that he existed solely in his own interior voice. Then he started up the stairs, carrying seabag and suitcase, guided up by the press of his companions, and as he went down a corridor toward the squad bay he passed an open office and Sergeant Hathaway entered his life: not a voice but a roar, and he turned and stood at attention, seabag and suitcase heavy in each hand, seeing now with vision narrowed and dimmed by fear the raging face, the pointing finger; and he tried for the voice to say Me, sir? but already Hathaway was coming toward him and with both fists struck his chest one short hard blow, the fists then open-

ing to grip his shirt and jerk him forward into the office; he heard
the shirt tear; somewhere outside the door he dropped his luggage;
perhaps they hit the door-jamb as he was going through, and he
stood at attention in the office; other men were there, his eyes were
aware of them but he was not, for in the cascade of curses from that
red and raging face he could feel and know only his fear: his body
was trembling, he knew as though he could see it that his face was
drained white, and now he had to form answers because the curses
were changing to questions, Hathaway's voice still at a roar, his
dark loathing eyes close to Paul's and at the same height; Paul told
him his name.

'Where did it happen?'

'Sir?'

'Where did she do it. Where the fuck were you *born*.'

'Lake Charles, Louisiana, sir.'

'Well no shit Lake Charles Louisiana sir, you college idiot, you
think I know where that is? Where is it?'

'South of New Orleans sir.'

'South of New Orleans. How *far* south.'

'About two hundred miles sir.'

'Well no shit. Are you a fucking fish? Answer me, candidate
shitbird. Are you a fucking fish?'

'No sir.'

'No sir. Why aren't you a fish?'

'I don't know sir.'

'You don't know. Well you better be a Goddamn fish because two
hundred miles south of New Orleans is in the Gulf of fucking
*Mex*ico.'

'West sir.'

'You said south. Are you calling me a liar, fartbreath? I'll break
your jaw. You know that? Do you *know* that?'

'Sir?'

'Do you know I can break your Goddamn jaw?'

'Yes sir.'

'Do you want me to?'

'No sir.'

'Why not? You can't use it. You can't Goddamn talk. If I had a
piece of gear that wasn't worth a shit and I didn't know how to use

it anyway I wouldn't give a good rat's ass if somebody broke it. Stop shaking. Who told you to wear that uniform? I said stop shaking.'

'My captain sir.'

'My *cap*tain. Who the fuck is your captain.'

'My reserve captain sir.'

'Is he a ragpicker?'

'Sir?'

'Is he a *rag*picker. How does he *eat.*'

'He has a hardware store, sir.'

'He's a ragpicker. Say it.'

'He's a ragpicker, sir.'

'I told you to stop shaking. Say my reserve captain is a ragpicker.'

'My reserve captain is a ragpicker, sir.'

Then the two fists came up again and struck his chest and gripped the shirt, shaking him back and forth, and stiff and quivering and with legs like weeds he had no balance, and when Hathaway shoved and released him he fell backward and crashed against a steel wall locker; then Hathaway had him pressed against it, holding the shirt again, banging him against the locker, yelling: 'You can't wear that uniform you shit you don't even know how to wear that uniform you wore it on the Goddamn plane playing Marine Goddamnit—Well you're not a Marine and you'll never be a Marine, you won't make it here one week, you will not be here for chow next Sunday, because you are a shit and I will break your ass in five days, I will break it so hard that for the rest of your miserable fucking life every time you see a man you'll crawl under a table and piss in your skivvies. Give me those emblems. Give them to me! Take them off, take them off, take them off—' Paul's hands rising first to the left collar, the hands trembling so that he could not hold the emblem and collar still, his right hand trying to remove the emblem while Hathaway's fists squeezed the shirt tight across his chest and slowly rocked him back and forth, the hands trembling; he was watching them and they couldn't do it, the fingers would not stop, they would not hold; then with a jerk and a shove Hathaway flung him against the locker, screaming at him; and he felt tears in his eyes, seemed to be watching the tears in his eyes, pleading with them to at least stay there and not stain his cheeks;

somewhere behind Hathaway the other men were still watching but they were a blur of khaki and flesh: he was enveloped and penetrated by Hathaway's screaming and he could see nothing in the world except his fingers working at the emblems.

Then it was over. The emblems were off, they were in Hathaway's hand, and he was out in the corridor, propelled to the door and thrown to the opposite wall with such speed that he did not even feel the movement: he only knew Hathaway's two hands, one at the back of his collar, one at the seat of his pants. He picked up his suitcase and seabag, and feeling bodiless as a cloud, he moved down the hall and into the lighted squad bay where the others were making bunks and hanging clothes in wall lockers and folding them into foot lockers, and he stood violated and stunned in the light. Then someone was helping him. Someone short and muscular and calm (it was Whalen), a quiet mid-western voice whose hand took the seabag and suitcase, whose head nodded for him to follow the quick athletic strides that led him to his bunk. Later that night he lay in the bunk and prayed dear please God please dear God may I have sugar in my blood. The next day the doctors would look at them and he must fail, he must go home; in his life he had been humiliated, but never never had anyone made his own flesh so uninhabitable. He must go home.

But his body failed him. It was healthy enough for them to keep it and torment it, but not strong enough, and each day he woke tired and rushed to the head where men crowded two or three deep at the mirrors to shave and others, already shaved, waited outside toilet stalls; then back to the squad bay to make his bunk, the blanket taut and without wrinkle, then running down the stairs and into the cool first light of day and, in formation with the others, he marched to chow where he ate huge meals because on the second day of training Hathaway had said: 'Little man, I want you to eat everything but the table cloth'; so on those mornings, not yet hungry, his stomach in fact near-queasy at the early morning smell of hot grease that reached him a block from the chow hall, he ate cereal and eggs and pancakes and toast and potatoes and milk, and the day began. Calisthenics and running in formation around the drill field, long runs whose distances and pace were at the whim of Lieutenant

Swenson, or the obstacle course, or assaulting hills or climbing the Hill Trail, and each day there came a point when his body gave out, became a witch's curse of one hundred and forty-five pounds of pain that he had to bear, and he would look over at Hugh Munson trying to do a push-up, his back arching, his belly drawn to the earth as though gravity had chosen him for an extra, jesting pull; at Hugh hanging from the chinning bar, his face contorted, his legs jerking, a man on a gibbet; at Hugh climbing the Hill Trail, his face pale and open-mouthed and dripping, the eyes showing pain and nothing more, his body swaying like a fighter senseless on his feet; at Hugh's arms taking him halfway up the rope and no more so he hung suspended like an exclamation point at the end of Hathaway's bellowing scorn.

In the squad bay they helped each other. Every Saturday morning there was a battalion inspection and on Friday nights, sometimes until three or four in the morning, Paul and Hugh worked together, rolling and unrolling and rolling again their shelter halves until, folded in a U, they fit perfectly on the haversacks which they had packed so neatly and squarely they resembled canvas boxes. They took apart their rifles and cleaned each part; in the head they scrubbed their cartridge belts with stiff brushes, then put them in the dryer in the laundry room downstairs; and they worked on shoes and boots, spit-shining the shoes and one pair of boots, and saddle-soaping a second pair of boots which they wore to the field; they washed their utility caps and sprayed them with starch and fitted them over tin cans so they would shape as they dried. And, while they worked, they drilled each other on the sort of questions they expected the battalion commander to ask. What *is* enfilade fire, candidate Hugh? Why that, colonel, is when the axis of fire coincides with the axis of the enemy. And can you name the chain of command as well? I can, my colonel, and, sorry to say, it begins with Ike. At night during the week and on Saturday afternoons they studied for exams. Hugh learned quickly to read maps and use the compass, and he helped Paul with these, spreading the map on his foot locker, talking, pointing, as Paul chewed his lip and frowned at the brown contour lines which were supposed to become, in his mind, hills and draws and ridges and cliffs. On Sunday afternoons they walked to the town of Quantico and, dressed in civilian clothes, drank beer incognito in bars filled with sergeants. Once they took the train to Washington and saw the Lincoln Memorial and pretended not to weep; then, proud of their legs and wind, they climbed the Washington Monument. One Saturday night they got happily and absolutely drunk in Quantico and walked home singing love songs.

Hugh slept in the bunk above Paul's. His father was dead, he lived with his mother and a younger sister, and at night in the squad bay he liked talking about his girl in Bronxville; on summer afternoons he and Molly took the train into New York.

'What do you do?' Paul said. He stood next to their bunk; Hugh sat on his, looking down at Paul; he wore a T-shirt, his bare arms were thin, and high on his cheekbones were sparse freckles.

'She takes me to museums a lot.'

'What kind of museums?'

'Art.'

'I've never been to one.'

'That's because you're from the south. I can see her now, standing in front of a painting. Oh Hugh, she'll say, and she'll grab my arm. Jesus.'

'Are you going to marry her?'

'In two years. She's a snapper like you, but hell I don't care. Sometimes I go to mass with her. She says I'll have to sign an agreement; I mean it's not *her* making me, and she's not bitchy about it; there's nothing she can do about it, that's all. You know, agree to raise the kids Catholics. That Nazi crap your Pope cooked up.'

'You don't mind?'

'Naw, it's *Mol*ly I want. *Her,* man—'

Now in his mind Paul was miles and months away from the squad bay and the smells of men and canvas and leather polish and gun oil, he was back in those nights last fall and winter and spring, showing her the stories he wrote, buying for her Hemingway's books, one at a time, chronologically, in hardcover; the books were for their library, his and Tommie's, after they were married; he did not tell her that. Because for a long time he did not know if she loved him. Her eyes said it, the glow in her cheeks said it, her voice said it. But she never did; not with her controlled embraces and kisses, and not with words. It was the words he wanted. It became an obsession: they drank and danced in night clubs, they saw movies, they spent hours parked in front of her house, and he told her his dreams and believed he was the only young man who had ever had such dreams and had ever told them to such a tender girl; but all this seemed incomplete because she didn't give him the words. Then one night in early summer she told him she loved him. She was a practical and headstrong girl; the next week she went to see a priest. He was young, supercilious, and sometimes snide. She spent an hour with him, most of it in anger, and that night she told Paul she must not see him again. She must not love him. She would not sign contracts. She spoke bitterly of incense and hocus-pocus and graven images. Standing at Hugh's bunk, remembering that long year of nights with Tommie, yearning again for the sound of his own voice, gently received, and the swelling of his heart as he told Tommie what he had to and wanted to be, he felt divided and perplexed; he looked at Hugh's face and thought of Molly's hand reaching out for that arm, holding it, drawing Hugh close to her as she gazed at a painting. He blinked his eyes, scratched his crew-cut head, returned to the squad bay with an exorcising wrench and a weary sigh.

'—Sometimes she lets me touch her, just the breasts you see, and that's fine, I don't push it. When she lets me I'm Goddamn *grate*ful. Jesus, you got to get a girl again. There's nothing like it. You know that? *Noth*ing. It's another world, man.'

On a hot grey afternoon he faced Hugh on the athletic field, both of them wearing gold football helmets, holding pugil sticks at the ready, as if they were rifles with fixed bayonets. Paul's fists gripped and encircled the smooth round wood; on either end of it was a large stuffed canvas cylinder; he looked into Hugh's eyes, felt the eyes of the circled platoon around him, and waited for Hathaway's signal to begin. When it came he slashed at Hugh's shoulder and neck but Hugh parried with the stick, then he jabbed twice at Hugh's face, backing him up, and swung the lower end of the stick around in a butt stroke that landed hard on Hugh's ribs; then with speed he didn't know he had he was jabbing Hugh's chest, Hathaway shouting now: 'That's it, little man: keep him going, keep him going; Munson get your balance, use your feet, Goddamnit—' driving Hugh back in a circle, smacking him hard on the helmeted ear; Hugh's face was flushed, his eyes betrayed, angry; Paul jabbing at those eyes, slashing at the head and neck, butt stroking hip and ribs, charging, keeping Hugh off balance so he could not hit back, could only hold his stick diagonally across his body, Paul feinting and working over and under and around the stick, his hands tingling with the blows he landed until Hathaway stopped him: 'All right, little man, that's enough; Carmichael and Vought, put on the headgear.'

Paul took off the helmet and handed it and the pugil stick to Carmichael. He picked up his cap from the grass; it lay next to Hugh's, and as he rose with it Hugh was beside him, stooping for his cap, murmuring: 'Jesus, you really like this shit, don't you.'

Paul watched Carmichael and Vought fighting, and pretended he hadn't heard. He felt Hugh standing beside him. Then he glanced at Hathaway, across the circle. Hathaway was watching him.

In the dark he was climbing the sixth and final hill, even the moon was gone, either hidden by trees or clouds or out of his vision because he was in such pain that he could see only that: his pain; the air was grey and heavy and humid, and he could not get enough of it; even as he inhaled his lungs demanded more and he exhaled with a rush and again drew in air, his mouth open, his throat and tongue dry, haunting his mind with images he could not escape: cold oranges, iced tea, lemonade, his canteen of water—He was falling back. He wasn't abreast of Whalen anymore, he was next to the man behind Whalen and then back to the third man, and he moaned and strove and achieved a semblance of a jog, a tottering climb away from the third man and past the second and up with Whalen again, then from behind people were yelling at him, or trying to, their voices diminished, choked off by their own demanding lungs: they were cursing him for lagging and then running to catch up, causing a gap which they had to close with their burning legs. Behind him Hugh was silent and Paul wondered if that silence was because of empathy or because Hugh was too tired to curse him aloud; he decided it was empathy and wished it were not.

And now Lieutenant Swenson reached the top, a tall helmeted

silhouette halted and waiting against the oppressive and mindless sky, and Paul's heart leaped in victory and resilience, he crested the hill, went happily past Swenson's panting and sweating face, plunged downward, leaning back, hard thighs and calves bouncing on the earth, then Swenson jogged past him, into the lead again and, walking now, brought them slowly down the hill and out of the trees, onto the wide quiet gravel road and again stepped aside and watched them go past, telling them quietly to close it up, close it up, you people, and Paul's stride was long and light and drunk with fatigue; he tried to punch Whalen's arm but couldn't reach him and didn't have the strength to veer from his course and do it—Then Swenson's voice high and clear: ''tawn: ten*buhn*,' and he straightened his back and with shoulders so tired and aching that he barely felt the cutting packstraps, he marched to Swenson's tenor cadence, loving now the triumphant rhythm of boots in loose gravel, cooling in his drying sweat, able now to think of water as a promise the night would keep. Then Swenson called out: 'Are you ready, Gunny?' and, from the rear, Hathaway's answering growl: 'Aye, Lieutenant—' and Paul's heart chilled, he had heard the mischievous threat in Swenson's voice and now it came: 'Dou-ble time—' a pause: crunching boots: groans, and then '—*buhn*.'

Swenson ran past him on long legs, swerved to the front of the two files, and slowed to a pace that already Paul knew he couldn't keep. For perhaps a quarter of a mile he ran step for step with Whalen, and then he was finished. His stride shortened and slowed. Whalen was ahead of him and he tried once to catch up, but as he lifted his legs they refused him, they came down slower, shorter, and falling back now he moved to his left so the men behind him could go on. For a moment he ran beside Hugh. Hugh jerked his pale face to the left, looked at him, tried to say something; then he was gone. Paul was running alone between the two files, they were moving past him, some spoke encouragement as they went—hang in there, man—then he was among the tall ones at the rear and still he was dropping back, then a strong hand extended from a gasping shadowed face and took his rifle and went on.

He did not look behind him but he knew: he could feel at his back the empty road, and he was dropping back into it when the last two men, flanking him, each took an arm and held him up. 'You can do it,' they said. 'Keep going,' they said. He ran with them. Vaguely above the sounds of his breathing he could hear the pain of others: the desperate breathing and always the sound of boots, not rhythmic now, for each man ran in step with his own struggle, but anyway steady, and that is what finally did him in: the endlessness of that sound. Hands were still holding his arms; he was held up and pulled forward, his head lolled, he felt his legs giving way, his arms, his shoulders, he was sinking, they were pulling him forward but he was sinking, his eyes closed, he saw red-laced black and then it was over, he was falling forward to the gravel, and then he struck it but not with his face: with his knees and arms and hands. Then his face settled forward onto the gravel. He was not unconscious, and he lay in a shameful moment of knowledge that he would remember for the rest of his life: he had quit before his body failed; the legs which now lay in the gravel still had strength which he could feel; and already, within this short respite, his lungs were ready again. They hurt, they labored, but they were ready.

'He passed out, sir.'

They were standing above him. The platoon was running up the road.

'Who is it?' Hathaway said.

'It's Clement, sir.'

'Leave his rifle here and you men catch up with the platoon.'

'Aye-aye, sir.'

There were two of them. They went up the road, running hard to catch up, and he wanted to tell them he was sorry he had lied, but he knew he never would. Then he heard or felt Hathaway squat beside him, the small strong hands took his shoulders and turned him over on his back and unbuckled his chin strap. He blinked up at Hathaway's eyes: they were concerned, interested yet distant, as though he were disassembling a weapon whose parts were new to him; and they were knowing too, as if he were not appraising the condition of Paul's body alone but the lack of will that had allowed it to fall behind, to give up a rifle, to crap out.

'What happened, Clement?'

'I don't know, sir. I blacked out.'

Hathaway's hands reached under Paul's hip, lifted him enough to twist the canteen around, open the flaps, pull it from the cover. The crunching of the platoon receded and was gone up the road in the dark. Hathaway handed him the canteen.

'Take two swallows.'

Paul lifted his head and drank.

'Now stand up.'

He stood, replaced the canteen on his hip, and buckled his chin strap. His shirt was soaked; under it the T-shirt clung to his back and chest.

'Here's your weapon.'

He took the M1 and slung it on his shoulder.

'Let's go,' Hathaway said, and started jogging up the road, Paul moving beside him, the fear starting again, touching his heart like a feather and draining his legs of their strength. But it didn't last. Within the first hundred yards it was gone, replaced by the quick-lunged leg-aching knowledge that there was no use being afraid because he knew, as he had known the instant his knees and hands and arms hit the gravel, that he was strong enough to make it; that Hathaway would not let him do anything but make it; and so his fear was impotent, it offered no chance of escape, and he ran now with Hathaway, mesmerized by his own despair. He tried to remember the road, how many bends there were, so he could look forward to that last curve which would disclose the lighted streets of what now felt like home. He could not remember how many curves there were. Then they rounded one and Hathaway said, 'Hold it,' and walked toward the edge of the road. Paul wiped sweat from his eyes, blinked them, and peered beyond Hathaway's back and shoulders at the black trees. He followed Hathaway and then he saw, at the side of the road, a man on his hands and knees. As he got closer he breathed the smell.

'Who is it?' Hathaway said.

'Munson.' His voice rose weakly from the smell. Paul moved closer and stood beside Hathaway, looking down at Hugh.

'Are you finished?' Hathaway said.

'I think so.'

'Then stand up.' His voice was low, near coaxing in its demand.

Hugh pushed himself up, stood, then retched again and leaned over the ditch and dry-heaved. When he was done he remained bent over the ditch, waiting. Then he picked up his rifle and stood straight, but he did not turn to face them. He took off his helmet and held it in front of him, down at his waist, took something from it, then one hand rose to his face. He was wiping it with a piece of toilet paper. He dropped the paper into the ditch, then turned and looked at Hathaway. Then he saw Paul, who was looking at Hugh's drained face and feeling it as if it were his own: the cool sweat, the raw sour throat.

'Man—' Hugh said, looking at Paul, his voice and eyes petulant; then he closed his eyes and shook his head.

'We'll run it in now,' Hathaway said.

Hugh opened his eyes.

'I threw up,' he said.

'And you're done.' Hathaway pointed up the road. 'And the barracks is that way.'

'I'll walk.'

'When you get back to New York you can do that, Munson. You can diddle your girl and puke on a six-pack and walk back to the frat house all you want. But here you run. Put on your helmet.'

Hugh slung his rifle on his shoulder and put his helmet on his head.

'Buckle it.'

He buckled it under his chin, then looked at Hathaway.

'I can't run. I threw up.' He gave Paul a weary glance, and looked up the road. 'It's not that I won't. I just can't, that's all.'

He stood looking at them. Then he reached back for his canteen, it rose pale in the moonlight, and he drank.

'All right, Munson: two swallows, then start walking; Clement, let's go.'

He looked at Hugh lowering the canteen, his head back gargling, then his eyes were on the road directly in front of him as he ran up a long stretch then rounded a curve and looked ahead and saw more of the road, the trees, and the black sky at the horizon; he was too tired to lift his head and see the moon and stars and this made him feel trapped on a road that would never end. Before the next curve he reached the point of fatigue he had surrendered to when he fell, and he moved through it into a new plane of struggle where he was certain that now his body would truly fail him, would fold and topple in spite of the volition Hathaway gave him. And then something else happened, something he had never experienced. Suddenly his legs told him they could go as far as he wanted them to. They did not care for his heat-aching head, for his thirst; they did not care for his pain. They told him this so strongly that he was frightened, as though his legs would force him to hang on as they spent the night jogging over Virginia hills; then he regained possession of them. They were his, they were running beside a man who had walked out of the Chosin Reservoir, and they were going to make it. When Paul turned the last bend and saw the street lights and brick buildings and the platoon, which had reached the blacktop road by the athletic field and was marching now, he felt both triumphant and disappointed: he wanted to show Hathaway he could keep going.

They left the gravel and now his feet pounded on the gift of smooth blacktop. They approached the platoon, then ran alongside it, and as they came abreast of Lieutenant Swenson, Hathaway said: 'Lieutenant, you better send a jeep back for Munson. Me and Clement's going to hit the grinder; we had a long rest up the road.' The lieutenant nodded. Paul and Hathaway passed the platoon and turned onto the blacktop parade field and started to circle it. It was a half-mile run. For a while Paul could hear Swenson's fading cadence, then it stopped and he knew Swenson was dismissing the platoon. In the silence of the night he ran alongside Hathaway, listened to Hathaway's breath and pounding feet, glanced at him, and looked up at the full moon over the woods. They left the parade field and jogged up the road between brick barracks until they reached Bravo Company and Hathaway stopped. Paul faced him and stood at attention. His legs felt like they were still running. He was breathing hard; he looked through burning sweat at Hathaway, also breathing fast and deep, his face dripping and red. Hathaway's eyes were not glaring, not even studying Paul; they seemed fixed instead on his own weariness.

'You get in the barracks, you get some salt tablets and you take 'em. I don't care if you've been drinking Goddamn Gulf water all your life. Dismissed.'

The rest of the platoon were in the showers. As he climbed the stairs he heard the spraying water, the tired, exultant, and ironic voices. In the corridor at the top of the stairs he stopped and looked at the full-length mirror, looked at his short lean body standing straight, the helmet on his head, the pack with a protruding bayonet handle, the rifle slung on his shoulder. His shirt and patches on his thighs were dark green with sweat. Then he moved on to the water fountain and took four salt tablets from the dispenser and swallowed them one at a time, tilting his head back to swallow, remembering the salt tablets on the construction job when he was sixteen and his father got him the job and drove him to work on the first day and introduced him to the foreman and said: 'Work him, Jesse; make a man of him.' Jesse was a quiet wiry Cajun; he nodded, told Paul to stow his lunch in the toolshed and get a pick and a spade. All morning he worked bare-headed under the hot June sun; he worked with the Negroes, digging a trench for the foundation, and at noon he was weak and nauseated and could not eat. He went behind the shed and lay in the shade. The Negroes watched him and asked him wasn't he going to eat. He told them he didn't feel like it. At one o'clock he was back in the trench, and thirty minutes later he looked up and saw his father in seersucker and straw hat standing with Jesse at the trench's edge. 'Come on up, son,' his father said. 'I'm all right,' and he lifted the pick and dropped more than drove it into the clay at his feet. 'You just need a hat, that's all,' his father said. 'Come on up, I'll buy you one and bring you back to work.' He laid the pick beside the trench, turned to the Negro working behind him, and said, 'I'll be right back.' 'Sure,' the Negro said. 'You get that hat.' He climbed out of the trench and walked quietly beside his father to the car. 'Jesse called me,' his father said in the car. 'He said the nigras told him you didn't eat lunch. It's just the sun, that's all. We'll get you a hat. Did you take salt tablets?' Paul said yes, he had. His father bought him a pith helmet and, at the soda fountain, a Seven-Up and a sandwich. 'Jesse said you didn't tell anybody you felt bad.' 'No,' Paul said. 'I didn't.' His father stirred his coffee, looked away. Paul could feel his father's shy pride and he loved it, but he was ashamed too, for when he had looked up and seen his father on the job, he had had a moment of hope when he thought his father had come to tenderly take him home.

By the time he got out of his gear and hung his wet uniform by the window and wiped his rifle clean and lightly oiled it, the rest of the platoon were out of the showers, most were in their bunks, and the lights would go out in five minutes. Paul went to the shower and stayed long under the hot spray, feeling the sweat and dirt leave him, and sleep rising through his aching legs, to his arms and shoulders, to all save his quick heart. He was drying himself when Whalen came in, wearing shorts, and stood at the urinal and looked over his shoulder at Paul.

'You and Hathaway run all the way in?'

'Yeah.'

'Then the grinder?'

Paul nodded.

'Good,' Whalen said, and turned back to the urinal. Paul looked at his strong, muscled wrestler's back and shoulders. When Whalen passed him going out, Paul swung lightly and punched his arm.

'See you in the morning,' he said.

The squad bay was dark when Paul entered with a towel around his waist. Already most of them were asleep, their breath shallow and slow. There was enough light from the corridor so he could see the rifle rack in the middle of the room, and the double bunks on either side, and the wall lockers against the walls. He went to his bunk. Hugh was sitting on the edge of it, his elbows on his knees, his forehead resting on his palms. His helmet and rifle and pack and cartridge belt were on the floor in front of his feet. He looked up, and Paul moved closer to him in the dark.

'How's it going,' he said softly.

'I threw *up*, man. You see what I mean? That's stupid, Goddamnit. For *what*. What's the point of doing something that makes you puke. I was going to keep running till the Goddamn stuff came up all over me. Is that smart, man?' Hugh stood; someone farther down stirred on his bunk; Hugh took Paul's arm and squeezed it; he smelled of sweat, his breath was sour, and he leaned close, lowering his voice. 'Then you crapped out and I thought good. *Good*, Goddamnit. And man I peeled off and went to the side of the road and waited for it to come up. Then I was going to find you and walk in and drink Goddamn water and piss in the road and piss on all of them.' He released Paul's arm. 'But that Goddamn Doberman pinscher made you run in. Jesus Christ what am I *do*ing here. What am I *do*ing here,' and he turned and struck his mattress, stood looking at his fist on the bed, then raised it and struck again. Paul's hand went up to touch Hugh's shoulder, but stopped in the space between them and fell back to his side. He did not speak either. He looked at Hugh's profiled staring face, then turned away and bent over his foot locker at the head of the bunk and took out a T-shirt and a pair of shorts, neatly folded. He put them on and sat on his locker while Hugh dropped his clothes to the floor and walked out of the squad bay, to the showers.

He got into the lower bunk and lay on his back, waiting for his muscles to relax and sleep to come. But he was still awake when Hugh came back and stepped over the gear on the floor and climbed into his bunk. He wanted to ask Hugh if he'd like him to clean his rifle, but he could not. He lay with aching legs and shoulders and back and arms, and gazed up at Hugh's bunk and listened to his shifting weight. Soon Hugh settled and breathed softly, in sleep. Paul lay awake, among silhouettes of bunks and wall lockers and rifle racks. They and the walls and the pale windows all seemed to breathe, and to exude the smells of men. Farther down the squad bay someone snored. Hugh murmured in his sleep, then was quiet again.

When the lights went on he exploded frightened out of sleep, swung his legs to the floor, and his foot landed on the stock of Hugh's rifle. He stepped over it and trotted to the head, shaved at a lavatory with Whalen, waited outside a toilet stall but the line was too long and with tightening bowels he returned to the squad bay. Hugh was lying on his bunk. Going past it to the wall locker he said: 'Hey Hugh. Hugh, reveille.' He opened his locker and then looked back; Hugh was awake, blinking, looking at the ceiling.

'Hugh—' Hugh did not look at him. 'Your *gear*, Hugh; what about your *gear*.'

He didn't move. Paul put on utilities and spit-shined boots and ran past him. At the door he stopped and looked back. The others were coming, tucking in shirts, putting on caps. Hugh was sitting on the edge of his bunk, watching them move toward the door. Outside the morning was still cool and Hathaway waited, his boots shining in the sunlight. The platoon formed in front of him and his head snapped toward the space beside Paul.

'Clement, did Munson Goddamn puke and die on the road last night?'

'He's coming, sir.'

'He's coming. Well no shit he's coming. What do you people think this is—Goddamn civilian life where everybody crosses the streets on his own time? A platoon is not out of the barracks until every member of that platoon is out of the barracks, and you people are not out of the barracks yet. You are still *in* there with—o-ho—' He was looking beyond them, at the barracks to their rear. 'Well now here he is. You people are here now. Munson, you asshole, come up here.' Paul heard Munson to his left, coming around the platoon; he walked slowly. He entered Paul's vision and Paul watched him going up to Hathaway and standing at attention.

'Well no shit Munson.' His voice was low. 'Well no shit now. Mr. Munson has joined us for chow. He slept a little late this morning. I understand, Munson. It tires a man out, riding home in a jeep. It gets a man tired, when he knows he's the only one who can't hack it. It sometimes gets him so tired he *doesn't even fucking shave*! Who do you think you are that you don't shave! I'll tell you who you are: you are *noth*ing you are *noth*ing you are *noth*ing. The best part of you dripped down your old man's *leg*!' Paul watched Hugh's flushed open-mouthed face; Hathaway's voice was lower now: 'Munson, do you know about the Goddamn elephants. Answer me Munson or I'll have you puking every piece of chow the Marine Corps feeds your ugly face. Elephants, Munson. Those big grey fuckers that live in the boondocks. They are like Marines, Munson. They stick with the herd. And if one of that herd fucks up in such a way as to piss off the rest of the herd, you know what they do to him? They exile that son of a bitch. They kick his ass out. You know what he does then? Son of a bitch gets lonesome. So everywhere the herd goes he is sure to follow. But they won't let him back in, Munson. So pretty soon he gets so lonesome he goes crazy and he starts running around the boondocks pulling up trees and stepping on troops and you have to go in and shoot him. Munson, you have fucked up my herd and I don't want your scrawny ass in it, so you are going to march thirty paces to the rear of this platoon. Now move out.'

'I'm going home.'

He left Hathaway and walked past the platoon.

'Munson!'

He stopped and turned around.

'I'm going home. I'm going to chow and then I'm going to see the chaplain and I'm going home.'

He turned and walked down the road, toward the chow hall.

'Munson!'

He did not look back. His hands were in his pockets, his head down; then he lifted it. He seemed to be sniffing the morning air. Hathaway's mouth was open, as though to yell again; then he turned to the platoon. He called them to attention and marched them down the road. Paul could see Hugh ahead of them, until he turned a corner around a building and was gone. Then Hathaway, in the rhythm of cadence, called again and again: 'You won't *talk* to Mun-son talk talk *talk* to Mun-son you won't *look* at Mun-son look look *look* at Mun-son—'

And, in the chow hall, no one did. Paul sat with the platoon, listened to them talking in low voices about Hugh and, because he couldn't see him, Hugh seemed to be everywhere, filling the chow hall.

Later that morning, at close order drill, the platoon was not balanced. Hugh had left a hole in the file, and Paul moved up to fill it, leaving the file one man short in the rear. Marching in fresh starched utilities, his cartridge belt brushed clean, his oiled rifle on his shoulder, and his boot heels jarring on the blacktop, he dissolved into unity with the rest of the platoon. Under the sun they sweated and drilled. The other three platoons of Bravo Company were drilling too, sergeants' voices lilted in the humid air, and Paul strode and pivoted and ignored the tickling sweat on his nose. Hathaway's cadence enveloped him within the clomping boots. His body flowed with the sounds. 'March from the waist down, people. Dig in your heels. That's it, people. Lean back. Swing your arms.

That's it, people—' With squared shoulders and sucked-in gut, his right elbow and bicep pressed tight against his ribs, his sweaty right palm gripping the rifle butt, Paul leaned back and marched, his eyes on the clipped hair and cap in front of him; certainty descended on him; warmly, like the morning sun.

Corporal of Artillery

A FTER THREE years, eleven months, and two days service, Corporal Fitzgerald re-enlisted for six years, collected a re-enlistment bonus and, that same afternoon, went to the bank in Oceanside and paid the balance of the note on his 1959 Chevrolet which was four years old. He had thought that would make him feel good, but it didn't. The balding man who took his money also took the pleasure, as though it hovered between them and the banker inhaled it and grinned before Fitzgerald had a chance. So he went home and paid the rest of the bills by mail: the hospital in San Diego, because the government would pay for your wife to have babies but not a nervous breakdown; the set of encyclopedias, and the revolving charge account which he had told Carol was supposed to revolve, not rocket. That had been for clothes and he realized when he wrote the check that he was paying ten per cent service charges. He walked to the corner and dropped the envelopes in the mail box, then stood there for a moment looking at the red and blue container of at least six years of his life (already knowing, though, that it was actually fifteen and a half, for if a man did ten years—halfway to retirement—he was a fool to get out). For a while he did not turn away from the mailbox. Even after being deprived at the bank, he had expected this final settling of accounts to yield a satisfaction which would carry him through at least the next two weeks in the desert. But he felt nothing. Or he would not acknowledge what he was beginning to feel. He read the times for mail pick-up and walked home to Carol, who seemed happy, free of burden.

For re-enlisting he rated thirty days leave, all at one shot, and the First Sergeant had even told him he could miss the two week firing exercise at 29 Palms. That was how happy the First Sergeant was;

he had been trying to fill the Battery's re-enlistment quota and he had worked on Fitzgerald for a long time: a series of what began as a rather formal interview in the First Sergeant's office, changed to friendly conversations on the drill field or atop some hill at Camp Pendleton, and evolved into fervid sermons, these occurring again behind the closed door of the office where First Sergeant Reichert—a slender man with a thick soft black moustache and a red dissipated face—asked him questions he could not answer and gave him answers he did not want and which he tried to resist. Fitzgerald had a whimsical variety of answers, but most frequently *I don't know*, to the recurring question: *What are you getting out FOR? What are you going to DO?*

Almost four years ago he had spurted into marriage: on leave in Bakersfield, after Boot Camp and infantry training, he had become convinced that he could not return to the Marines without Carol. So he had brought her along, finding himself after bare transition the head of a household, and easily and amazingly enough able to feed his wife and himself as well as the three children who came as steadily as the combination of Carol and diaphragm failed to work. He had counted on his breadwinning lasting forever, though he was uncertain about what form it would take. As the expiration of his enlistment drew near, First Sergeant Reichert stepped in with the disrupting ability to convince him—for hours and sometimes days at a time—that his life was comfortably made for him, that it could never get better than it was now. Reichert finally won by writing the sum of Fitzgerald's debts on one scrap of paper and his re-enlistment bonus—fourteen hundred and forty dollars—on another, then dangling them over his desk, crumpling them together with a clap of his hands, throwing the ball of paper into the wastebasket, and saying: *You see? Redemption, lad, redemption.*

Besides that, he could go to Bakersfield next day and forget about 29 Palms. But Fitzgerald had been smart about taking leave: he told the First Sergeant he would wait until payday, the week after the firing exercise. He did not tell the First Sergeant, or Carol either, that if he went home right after shipping over he wouldn't want to come back. And with Feeney there maybe he just by God wouldn't.

There were a lot of things he didn't tell Carol because she was finally a good girl and it wasn't her fault. Even during her bad time, she had chosen as her targets the children and the people who wanted the bills paid, leaving him fairly unscathed. Or most of the time. Still he was a little tough on her the morning after his re-enlistment, when he woke knowing he had to get aboard a truck and ride out to 29 Palms for two weeks of Mickey Mouse. She got up before he did and put on make-up. While he was eating buckwheat cakes, she woke the children and they all got in the car to drive him to the barracks. It touched him that Carol was looking pretty just to feed him and drive him in and he wondered if she'd still do that six years from now, in 1969, when—if he was very lucky—he might be a staff sergeant. He decided she wouldn't, so now her face and hair and smell only annoyed him. As she turned into the Battery parking lot, he said: 'Look: it's just two weeks. Anybody comes around selling encyclopedias for kids that can't read, you lock the door.'

'That's not fair.'

'It's expensive and it's paid for.'

'Well he *did* make me feel like a bad mother.'

'Yeah: well you're not, so let's learn from experience. I learn, and I'm just twenty-two years old. That's what everybody keeps forgetting around here.'

She was hurt instead of angry and, once in the truck, he was sorry. In that evening's sunset he squatted outside his tent and wrote her a letter. She answered by return mail and they were all right again.

He was a scout-observer for a forward observation team, so he spent the entire two weeks in the desert sitting on steep hills of loose rock, his lips chapping, his face burning, though it would not change color for it was densely freckled. He and the lieutenant took turns calling in fire missions, adjusting the 105 Howitzers on imaginary targets: convoys of trucks, tanks, gun emplacements, and columns of advancing troops. He got through the two weeks without making any mistakes, and on the final evening he sat on a small rock at the base camp, his metal tray of food resting across his knees. The camp was in a horseshoe of low cliffs which were beginning to turn purple in the sunset. At one end, the officers' large pyramidal tents were in line on a rise of sand overlooking the rest of the camp. The lower walls of these tents were uniformly rolled up and, when he looked up there once, he could see the cots inside. Below the officers' area were the Staff NCOs' pyramidals and the troops' tents.

He ate everything on his tray. It was too much and he did not particularly enjoy its taste, but the meal was something he deserved at the end of the firing exercise. When he finished he smoked a Camel, thinking that was one commercial that didn't lie, then he field-stripped it, rose lethargically, and joined the line of troops waiting to clean their trays. Then he walked slowly over deep yielding sand, back to his tent. The cliffs were dark purple now and the camp was in their shadow.

His tent was waist-high. On hands and knees he crawled through the opening, squeezing past the tent pole, then squatted to brush off his trousers before lying on his outstretched sleeping bag, which was zipped against sand and dust. Thorton was lying opposite him, almost as near as Carol in the double bed at home.

'Duty on the moon,' Thorton said. 'Nothing growing, nothing moving.'

He had said that about a dozen times in the last two weeks.

'Nothing but Marines,' Fitzgerald said.

'Like I said: nothing. Got a cigarette?'

'Not for a short-timer.'

He tossed his pack onto Thorton's chest.

'Why don't I just keep 'em?'

'Go ahead. I got two more packs.'

'Call me when your hitch is up, and I'll put you on the payroll.'

'What payroll?'

'I don't know.'

'You better find out fast, before the First Sergeant gets you.'

Thorton sat up and folded his arms on his knees.

'When my hitch is up,' Fitzgerald said, 'I'll ship for six more.'

'Okay, John Wayne.'

'I'd be throwing ten years away.'

'If you can take twenty years of this, lots o' luck.'

'Nineteen and a half.'

Then it was dark outside. Breathing the smells of dust and canvas, Fitzgerald made desultory conversation with Thorton: cursing by rote sand and chapped lips, conjuring a shower hot at first then cold; and they talked about Gunny Palenski whom they at once liked and hated, and beer from the very bottom of a chest of ice, and girls in the back seats of cars. They had said all this nearly every night, and they realized it together and stopped. Fitzgerald sat up, took off his boots and shirt and trousers, and squirmed into his sleeping bag; he left it unzipped, lying on his back, looking up at the tent wall sloping across his face.

Reveille—Gunny Palenski's hoarse raging voice—was at five o'clock Friday morning; he woke and stared at the forward tent pole outlined against pre-dawn light at the tent's opening. Some time during the night he had zipped his sleeping bag and now he did not want to get up into the gelid morning and shave with cold water and stand in line for chow; he smelled hot grease from the field galley and tried not to think of those fried eggs turning cool on his tray quicker than he could eat them. He knew one thing: for a month or even two after he retired he would sleep late, getting up about ten or whenever his body refused to stay in bed any longer, putting on a T-shirt and khakis, drinking coffee for a while, maybe shaving, maybe not. Then he would get a job, having had that space of slow mornings when there was no ringing clock to force him out of bed and into uniform while Carol was sleep-walking in the kitchen, pushing himself to the table and eating because he had to, just as he made himself go to the barracks for another day of sometimes doing nothing, not one damned thing, and on other days people ran around and hollered at you until you wanted to kick over all the bunks and wall lockers and set the place on fire. He looked over at Thorton who had closed his eyes again and said:

'Let's hit it.'

They got up, dressed quickly, rolled up their sleeping bags, took the tent down and helped each other fold the shelter halves into U-shaped blanket rolls which they strapped to their field marching packs. Fitzgerald laid the packs side by side and placed their helmets on top of them; then he and Thorton walked to chow, passing troops who cursed and panted as they broke their tents; to the east, a smear of rose-colored light showed over the hills.

'First ones finished,' Thorton said.

'Goddamn right.'

When they reached Camp Pendleton in late afternoon, Carol was waiting in the parking lot. The red Chevrolet was shining, its grill and hood seeming to show off for him as he approached. From the back seat Mike and Susan were calling him. He got in, leaned over Jerry in the car seat, and kissed Carol; all of it happened so fast and awkwardly that he didn't really see her, so he pulled away. She was wearing a pink dress, her blonde hair was shorter, and its dark streaks had disappeared.

'I washed the car,' she said. 'And I got my hair done.'

'It looks great.'

'The car or my hair?'

'Both. I meant the hair.'

She smiled at him and backed out of the parking lot. Mike, who was three and the oldest child, said:

'You buy me gum?'

'Daddy didn't go to the store,' Fitzgerald said. With his left hand he was touching Mike and Susan: rubbing their shoulders, stroking their heads; but he was looking at Carol.

'You've been sunbathing,' he said.

'Every day.'

'All over?'

'Just what you see.'

'I want to see the rest.'

'It won't be long,' she said. 'I didn't give them naps, except Jerry.'

Mike and Jerry were blond, but Susan had red hair like his and, so far, she had been spared his freckles. He sank a little in the seat and smiled at that splash of color in one family.

'How was it?' Carol said.

'All right. They brought beer out last Sunday and we played volleyball.'

'Did you have enough money?'

'I had two bucks and I got one off Thorton. I wasn't going to shave that day, but the Gunny caught me and reamed me out.'

'He *did*?'

'I told him to shove it up his ass.'

She grinned suddenly. She always got tickled when he talked that way, and once in a while after a beer or two she'd try to say something nasty-funny. She had told him it was nice, knowing that nobody could tell you how to talk, and he thought that was funny and sort of sad too, as though she were playing grown-up when here she was with three kids and not even old enough to vote yet. Not that he had ever voted, or ever would either. He never got the word on what those politicians were talking about and he didn't believe them anyway.

'You see that doctor again?'

'Just once. He said I won't have to see him much longer, 'cause the birth control pills will help me relax.'

'Good.'

'You don't mind about my hair, do you?'

'Long as you had the money. It looks good.'

'I got groceries and cigarettes till payday and filled the car and opened a charge account at the drug store so I can get tranquilizers and the pills. Did I leave anything out?'

He was going to say something about the charge account, but he remembered how she was before and now it looked like she'd be all right, so he let it pass.

'Beer,' he said. 'Did you get beer?'

'A whole case.' She sounded so pleased that he felt sorry for her. 'And I put a six-pack in the refrigerator.'

'Three apiece.'

'What?'

'It's four days till payday, so we get three apiece a day.'

'Oh.'

They lived in a government housing area in Oceanside: two-storied red brick buildings, with grey roads curving in from the highway then out again, paved oxbows which existed to get Marines to and from the Base. Fitzgerald took a long shower, just the way he and Thorton had talked about it; when he finished, Jerry was in the playpen and Mike and Susan were watching cartoons. Carol opened two beers and they went outside, sitting on a slab of concrete they called the porch. They sat close to each other, their bare feet on a patch of dirt where the grass had died. Just over the roofs across the street, the sun was falling toward the ocean they could not see.

'We'll get to Bakersfield Tuesday evening,' Fitzgerald said. 'Wednesday we'll have everybody out to my place, starting at noon.'

'*Can* we?'

'Sure. The old man'll like that.'

'I wonder what they're all doing now.'

'Same old things.'

He smiled, thinking of big crazy Feeney with a beer in his fist and a long narrow cigar between his teeth.

'Except Feeney,' he said. 'He's probably thought up something different.'

'You think he's still there?'

'Feeney? Sure he's there.'

'I love that silly man.'

'Yeah, well don't tell *him* that.'

'I didn't mean that way.'

'I know.'

She lit a cigarette and he watched her fingers: they were deliberate and steady.

'You take a tranquilizer today?'

'Not a one.'

He patted her knee.

'You won't tell anybody at home, will you?' she said.

'Nobody's business.'

'I'll be so glad to see Vicki, I'll probably tell her myself.'

He went inside and got two more beers, then listened quietly as she talked about her visit to the doctor, and going to the beach with Cathy Thorton, and how the kids had behaved without him. Then he said: 'About that charge account. Let's close it.'

From the corner of his eye he watched her jaws tighten on whatever it was she had to hold back.

'Okay,' she said. 'I don't need tranquilizers much more anyway and I can stock up on the pills on paydays.'

'Sure. It'll work out.'

'I don't know how you close one. Do you just walk in and say I want to close my account?'

'I don't know either, but I'll find out tomorrow. You remember

Feeney shoplifting? The time he got brassieres 'cause he said everything else was guarded?'

She was laughing now.

'I bet he just wanted them,' she said.

'Not Feeney: he didn't have to steal 'em. Suppose I don't shave
all week-end.'

'I don't care.'

'It's not enough to scratch anyway.'

'Yes it is, but I never feel it.'

She pressed her leg against his.

'Is that right?' he said.

'That's right. I missed you.'

'I got kinda tired of Thorton too. Okay: I won't shave till
Monday. I'll get in shape for Bakersfield. Maybe I won't stick to it,
but I'm planning on not shaving for thirty days.'

'Don't. Grow a red beard.'

'It'd take me three months, but I'll get some itchy fuzz. And we'll
tell the folks we want my old room so the sun won't come in and
every morning we'll by God sleep till we can't sleep anymore. And
they better not bust in on us either, 'cause they might get embarrassed.'

'It'll be safe too.'

'Damn right. Do they make you sick?'

'No. I'm not gaining weight either.'

She stood up.

'I have to start dinner.'

'Hell with it. Let's sit here till dark then we'll pick up some
hamburgers and go to the drive-in.'

'What's on?'

'Who cares? How 'bout a beer while you're up.'

'Your last one?'

'Nope. We'll drink as much as we want then buy some more.'

At dark they reached the movie—a musical—and Fitzgerald said:
Anyway, it's not *The Sands of Iwo Goddamn Jima* and Carol laughed
and unwrapped his hamburger for him. Soon the children were
sleeping on the back seat. The movie was all right but Fitzgerald
didn't care much for Debbie Reynolds and he grew restless, looking
into the cars around him until he could see nothing but silhouettes.

He slid down in the seat, watching Debbie through the steering wheel. and remembered he and Carol going to the drive-in at Bakersfield, sometimes with Feeney and that wild black-haired girl, whatever her name was, but most of the time alone.

'We never saw the movies,' he said.

'What movies?'

'At home.'

'Not many,' she said, and he could hear the grin in her voice.

'Remember—what was the name of it? When it rained?'

'*Marjorie Morningstar*,' she said.

She slid close to him and he put his arm around her.

'Vicki told me it was so good, and I wanted to see it,' she said.

'It was the rain. Everybody was staying in their cars and you couldn't see much through the windows.'

'It wasn't the rain. It was you.'

'I wanted my clothes off.'

'So did I,' she said.

'We could've got caught anyway, naked during the whole movie, and I bet we did it more times than Natalie Wood.'

'Because we really did it. You want to go home now?'

'Don't you want to see the rest?' he said. 'I thought you liked it.'

'Not anymore. Let's go.'

He lifted the speaker off his window and hung it up outside.

'We'll have to be careful when we carry the kids in,' she said.

'They won't wake up. You sure you don't want to see the rest?'

'If you don't hurry and take us home, it'll be just like Bakersfield.'

He drove home and carried each child to bed; none of them stirred. He tiptoed out of their bedroom and into his own, where Carol waited in the dark. She lifted her arms to him as, undressing, he stared at the stretch of white between her tan shoulders and legs. But it was over in a rush, before he had even got started. After that he slept badly. At half past two by the bedside clock he woke, his palms pressing against the mattress as though to push him upright. For a moment he thought he was back in the desert. Then he turned to Carol and, silently, with quick hands, he pulled her out of sleep. This time it took longer and he was able to marvel and anticipate and remember all at once, recalling the first time parked right in front of her house, the porch light watching them but they were safe down in the darkness of the seat and anyway it was late, her parents were asleep, and anyway it happened so fast they hadn't worried about anything except letting it happen, then she had sighed, peaceful, relieved, and said *We finally did it* and squeezed him till he grunted; after that it was all the time and they even had a bed when she was babysitting, and once the Heatheringtons had come home early so he had to escape through the bedroom window, unbuckled, shoes in hand, leaving her to smooth the bed, her skirt, and her face before fleeing to a lighted part of the house; best of all was home on that first leave, pulsating with four months' absence, and they had spent entire afternoons on a blanket in the woods—

Now he fell away from her, sprawled and grateful and silent, his body sinking into the mattress, into a heavy sleep that lasted until almost noon. He woke to the sound of Carol's voice in the living room. She was talking on the phone, telling someone—probably Cathy Thorton—about going to Bakersfield.

'It'll be like a honeymoon,' she said. 'What? Oh they're *great*. You ought to take 'em—they don't make you sick or anything, you just have to remember to take 'em. Uh-uh, not a pound. Really, they're great—'

She sounded very happy and he was not ready for that—not right now—so when she hung up and came toward the bedroom he closed his eyes and pretended he was asleep.

The Shooting

THE GUN FIGHT between the sailor and the Marine riot squad was in a Navy housing area on the base, so the civilian police were not involved, and during much of the fight Sergeant Chuck Everett was in sole command. Moments after the fight ended, a Navy photographer took a picture of Sergeant Everett; two days later the picture was on the front page of the local newspaper, a weekly which reported the news of Oak Harbor for its thirty-five hundred citizens. Except for occasional accidents (a curving road, treacherous to drunks, led north from the town to Deception Pass, where a high bridge crossed the water from Whidbey Island to the mainland), the newspaper's tragedies were drawn from the Naval Air Station: a year ago a bomber had crashed on Olympic Peninsula; three months ago another had gone into the cold sea off Puget Sound. The story of the gun fight was the first of its kind.

Chuck Everett was twenty-five years old, in his seventh year of peacetime service; he was a large man with a wide face that always looked sunburned, though at Whidbey Island there was more rain than sun, more grey than blue. Every Thursday he went to the Post Exchange and got a crewcut. At the Marine Barracks he worked as a Sergeant of the Guard, rotating the duty with two other sergeants. It was a good job, and he didn't mind when his duty came every third day. On those nights he inspected posts between midnight and dawn. There were twelve posts, some on the west side of the island, some on the east side. Crossing the island, he drove through Oak Harbor; at that time of night the town was silent, and he could hear only the engine of his pick-up, and the sound of its tires on the pavement, which was usually wet from fog. He liked driving through town, liked to wonder if all those civilians were asleep or if maybe some of them were up to a little hanky-pank. It took him over an hour to inspect all the sentries, and as he drove he often daydreamed about things whose details he could not recall the next day. He could only remember having a pleasant drive in the wet sea-smelling air.

There were other nights, though, when he felt a vague restless-ness, and he thought about girls. One April night a month before the gunfight, he went to see Toni. Her husband was with a bomber squadron on a carrier in the Pacific. She lived in a fourplex, in Navy housing just off the base, up the road from the main gate. The Navy Shore Patrol would be out in their truck, and if they saw his pick-up at Toni's, he'd get busted to corporal at the very least. He was both scared and excited, and as he turned off the headlights and drove slowly down her street, he wondered if he'd be able to get one up, and he remembered one of his favorite pieces ever, when he was a senior in high school and he and Loretta Cain had one schoolday afternoon sneaked into a storage compartment for athletic equipment. It was under the bleachers in the gym, there was a lot of floor space, and you could walk in it if you bent nearly double. Its only door opened onto the gym floor. Chuck and Loretta lay on a wrestling mat among basketballs, volley balls, tackling dummies and the smell of old sweat. They were just getting started when a p.e. class came in to play basketball. Chuck paused and listened to the dribbling, the shouts, the whistle. Then he went ahead and did it.

Now he parked down the street from Toni's, realizing as he walked back to her house that the truck's exact location didn't matter, that if the Shore Patrol saw it anywhere in Navy housing he would have to make up one hell of a story. Then he wondered how loud he'd have to knock to wake her up. He was in luck. There was a light on at the back of the house, in the kitchen; he went to the back door and watched her putting dishes away, a sixteen-ounce Hamm's on the kitchen table and a burning cigarette in the ash tray. He waited to see if another Hamm's would come in from the living room, with a man holding it. When he thought she was alone he tapped the glass and her shoulders jerked, then she saw him and was frightened and surprised and pleased all at once. She didn't look caught, though, so he knew it was all right. He didn't think she was playing around, but you had to figure if a married woman would go with you, she'd go with another. She had a chain lock on the door and as she worked it she started to giggle, a fine-looking dark little girl, not twenty yet, alone at one-thirty in the morning but still her hair combed and some lipstick left, and he thought what a good idea this was. She spoke in a laughing whisper: 'What are you *doing*?'

'Patrolling,' he said, and grinned and shut the door. 'How come you're awake?'

'Johnny Carson.' She stepped back and cocked her head, hands on her hips, playing wife with him. 'You crazy man. Want a beer?'

'Nope,' he said. 'I'm on duty.'

Then he was laughing and she was too, but she stopped when he took off his cap, careful not to touch its spit-shined visor, and laid it on the table; then he unbuckled his white web pistol belt and lowered it to a chair. By the time he got to the buttons of his battle jacket she was pulling her blouse out of her Levis and walking away from him, past the room where the child was sleeping, to the bedroom. When he finished he drove to the Shore Patrol office and had a cup of coffee with the sailors.

T HE SAILOR, they said afterward, had always been funny. Someone remembered that he never laughed much. Someone else remembered that he never talked much either. The Senior Medical Officer gave the final opinion. He was a bear-shaped captain, perhaps the only officer in the Navy who had taken advantage of an old regulation allowing beards: his was red and bushy. He had considerable wit, a large and colorful vocabulary, and he loved to talk, to lead a conversation to some strange point which existed largely for his own amusement, then to end it with a deep laugh, a slap on the shoulder, the ordering of another round. His fellow officers liked to listen to him, to quote him, to retell his stories; but his beard, his diction, his playfulness, kept them instinctively on guard. This captain read a copy of the investigation, pulled at his beard, and said Philip Korsmeyer had probably had a passive-aggressive reaction to service life in general and to his new role as a husband and nascent father. Everyone else, or at least everyone who by that time was still interested, readily agreed that this was so.

The written report of the investigation—original and five copies—had the appearance or at least the heft of finality. There were statements by an ensign and chief petty officer who commanded Korsmeyer's division. They said he was quiet, did his job, never caused any trouble; yet there had been, they felt, something different about him. From the six members of the Marine riot squad came six statements which all, in their repetition, presented a rock-like segment of truth: when the Corporal of the Guard sounded the buzzer they reported to his desk; he told them this was the real thing, issued them ammunition for the four riot guns and two M1's, and sent them by truck to the housing area, where Corporal Visconti deployed them for a fire fight with someone whom they couldn't see and didn't shoot at anyway, the fire fight being led by Sergeant Everett and, later, Captain Melko.

There were also statements by a sailor and his wife, who lived next door to the Korsmeyers; Mary Korsmeyer had used their phone to call the Marine Barracks. The longest statements were by Mary Korsmeyer, Captain Melko, and Sergeant Everett. The Commanding Officer of the Marine Barracks, a major, was mostly concerned with the statements of Captain Melko and Sergeant Everett; for there was the question of a cease fire order having gone unheard. The Major was not entirely satisfied with the opinion of the investigating officer, a lieutenant-commander, who concluded that 'in the heat of battle, Sergeant Everett did not hear Captain Melko's order to cease fire.' Except for an interest in the story itself, the Senior Medical Officer found that Mary Korsmeyer's statement was the only one useful to him. It was from this statement that he decided what had been wrong with Philip Korsmeyer.

Phil Korsmeyer himself did not know what was wrong, though for a month or so he knew something terribly strange was happening to him, and he also knew that it was terribly unique: that his friends in the squadron and his plump sweet Mary were not the sort of people who were visited by such nightmares, which were fearfully repetitious so that some mornings after a free night he woke relieved, but brave and curious enough to lie there for a while and try to remember if perhaps he had had the dream after all and had forgotten it. While Mary made breakfast he lay with his eyes closed, trying to force his mind back into the mysteries of night and sleep; then, satisfied that he had been spared for a night, he would get up and dress with the hope that whatever it was had left him forever.

After two months his hope became desperate, he started smoking before breakfast, and he was doing a couple of things that Mary called a nervous habit and which she said made her nervous too. He pinched his cheek while they talked over soiled plates at the dinner table, and he did a lot of pacing in the living room, his hands in his pockets, his shoulders slumped. They were six months married and she was three months pregnant and she thought he was nervous about being a father and maybe a husband as well. He was twenty years old, tall and slender, and she had believed that marriage would fill him out (it was what her mother told her), but instead he seemed to be getting thinner. Or maybe she only thought so because, with her baby, she was gaining weight.

About two weeks before the gun fight he became very quiet, distracted; when she asked if he wanted to try another channel or what he wanted to eat, he wouldn't answer. At first she simply asked him again in a louder voice. But after a few days she was certain that he regretted her pregnancy and therefore their life together. So one night when she asked him to throw her the cigarettes and he kept staring at the television, she said 'Hey!' and loudly clapped her hands. His face jerked at her, his eyes returning in a startled instant from that fearful distance. She left the room and he followed her. She stood at the kitchen sink, gulping milky water from a glass unwashed since dinner, looking out the window at the dark, while he asked her what was wrong.

'You don't love me,' she said.

He tried to soothe her, but his hands on her shoulders and arms were no more intimate than the brushing touch of a stranger on a bus.

Phil's dream was this: six people (he finally got their number straight) came for him and carried him alive to his grave. They took him from a bed and a room of eclectic familiarity: he could not recall these in detail, but in his daylight memory he felt that the bed was from some other house and time in his life, the enclosing walls and ceiling from another. He thought some of the people were women, but their bodies were vague or robed—he didn't know which—and their faces were merely shapes without features. They lifted him from the bed and all at once he was in a dark cemetery, and above the staring faces were black crowns of trees. They always brought him to the edge of a grave whose waiting depth he sensed yet never saw, for he was looking up at them, pleading with them and sometimes asking who they were and why were they doing this to him, but he never knew whether all his questions and pleas were only in his mind and for some reason not being voiced, or if he was indeed talking aloud and they were simply ignoring him. In any case, they never seemed to hear. They spoke to him, though, but he wasn't sure what they said. Remembering—next morning, afternoon, evening, night—he thought they only said one or two words at odd and meaningless intervals.

Then on a foggy Monday morning in May, two days before he went (as the Navy doctor and the newspaper said) berserk, he learned what they were saying at night. He had just stepped out of the shower, dried himself, put on his shorts, and stood at the steamed mirror; he was wiping it so he could shave when he heard the voice behind him, at the toilet. It said *Yes*. He spun around, already knowing his eyes were useless for something like this.

For the next two days he heard the voices, fought them, tried to get back to the far-off land he had left behind, so that sometimes he knew quite clearly that he loved his wife, he was looking forward with curiosity to the birth of a child, he had only one more year to do in the Navy, and he had a job waiting in his uncle's auto body shop in Eugene, Oregon. He saw all this, knew it to be true, knew that if he could rid himself of the voices of night he could return to those modest yet pleasurable expectancies of his days. But this knowledge came to him only in moments which were more and more separated until, watching television Wednesday night, he suddenly rose, upsetting an ash tray from the arm of his chair, and went quickly to the kitchen: not running only because there wasn't enough room, for he wanted to run—fear at first, then a sense of victorious flight, of ultimate purpose, having left the voices in the room with the television, though as he jerked open the kitchen drawer and fumbled for a handle, any handle of any knife, they were after him again, at his back in the kitchen: *Yes—Well: you, surely—Yes*; and he got the paring knife and slashed then sawed at his wrist, the knife had always been dull, then Mary was there, moving at him, reaching for him, and he slashed at her too, missing the breasts, and she turned screaming and ran from the house.

The knife had done little: three cuts, like the footprint of a bird, were scratched near bloodlessly into the pale underside of his left wrist. He laid the knife on the stove and stood holding his wrist, though still there was only enough blood to cover the scratches. He wished he hadn't struck at Mary, he wished she hadn't run out, and he wished with all his heart she would come back; yet at the core of his despair, of his knowledge that she was never coming back, there opened for him a despair so ultimate that it gave him hope: abandoned forever, beset by the shades who quietly watched him now from some point which was in his mind yet in the kitchen too—by the refrigerator or stove—so his mind was the kitchen and the kitchen his mind, he now saw that he was about to escape forever. He would move out of this network of betrayal and attack, he would ascend crashing through the night. It was motion he wanted now, and though he was weeping and actually moaning (he hadn't known that for a minute or two), there was an affirmative briskness in his steps through the living room, three paces down the hall, left into the bedroom where he switched on the overhead light, glancing at the bed covered by a green spread, and at the bedside table which held Mary's *Redbook* and package of Rolaids. He took the .22 rifle from the closet and sat on the bed to load the tubular magazine. After inserting four rounds he realized that was three more than he needed, but he liked the joke, liked sitting there in the middle of this joke that was in the middle of the swirl of devils and Mary's reaching hands and the silence that felt like chaotic voices, as though he sat dying and unnoticed at a party of strange drunks. So he kept loading until the magazine was filled. He was considering trying for the heart or sticking the barrel in his mouth when he heard the siren, then an abrupt squeal of tires outside his house.

He rose and turned out the light; when he again faced the room there was a dull flashing red light breaking the shadows, reflected from the walls. Going to the open window he saw the truck, the blinking light atop its cab, and now entering the lawn a Marine wearing a white belt. Phil shot twice from the hip and the Marine scuttled away into the dark of the lawn or the road. Watching the window as if not a bullet but a man might come through, Phil moved backwards around the bed and pushed it against the wall beneath the windows. Then the bullets came: twice the blaze and report of a .45, shattering a raised window, cracking into the wall behind him. He fired several shots at the truck, then kneeling at the bed as in prayer, his chin on the mattress, the rifle resting across it, he waited.

CROUCHED behind the fender, Chuck wished he had his deer rifle, his Winchester .30-.30 that he kept in the Barracks armory. With the first two shots from the house he had crawled into the truck and, with the brake and clutch pedals jamming his ribs, he had radioed the Corporal of the Guard, then switched off the blinking red light. Now there was nothing to do but wait for the riot squad.

They got there quickly, just as in drills, and he watched proudly as the panel truck halted a block away, the riot squad running low from the rear of the truck, spreading out as they crossed the road to the lawns and went down on their bellies, weapons thumping and rattling as they struck the earth. Chuck yelled for Visconti, and after a few moments saw him crawling in the shadow of a darkened house, and for the first time he realized that in all these dark houses people were watching, their faces exposed just enough so they could see out the windows. When Visconti reached a point where the truck was between him and the sailor's house, he sprinted across the road, bent low, his rifle at port, then squatted beside Chuck who saw the scene as a blending of his infantry training and movies of World War II.

'Gimmee the rifle,' he said.

Visconti gave it to him.

'The belt too. Okay. Here's what you do—' As he spoke he took clips from the pouches and, reaching up, placed them on the fender. He told Visconti to send two men to the rear of the house, that they would take cover and wait, and if the sailor ran out, they would shoot him. Then he gave Visconti the .45 and told him to bring the other three troops back to the truck, where they would set up a base of fire on the house while he and Visconti assaulted it.

'Jesus Christ,' Visconti said.

'You got it?'

Visconti nodded and told it back to him while Chuck, on one knee, pulled back the M1's bolt a couple of inches, glanced down in the dark at the dull yellow of the chambered brass cartridge, and eased the bolt forward again. Then he fired eight quick rounds over the hood; as he ducked again, one sweeping hand brought a new clip from the fender. Visconti was gone. Chuck waited for return fire from the window, but there was none. He watched the troops crawl into a cluster around Visconti three lawns away; after what seemed a long time for such simple orders, two men broke the cluster, rose and sprinted across the road. Chuck gave them two minutes to get behind the house, then he emptied three clips at the windows, remembering this time to sweep from left to right, aiming low. Still the sailor did not fire. He looked around, spotted his cap beside the truck, put it on the rifle's muzzle, steadied it so the visor pointed forward, then slowly raised it. Two slugs plunked into the hood and he jerked the rifle so the cap fell; then turning to pick it up he looked into the face of Captain Melko, bareheaded, his face tense but competent, the pale silver bars on his collar and epaulets already speaking for the silent man who wore them, relieving Chuck of command.

'Did they bring tear gas?' Melko said.

'No sir.'

Melko shut his lips impatiently; he opened the truck door and crawled in. While he was talking on the radio, Visconti shouted 'Cover us!' and Chuck fired while they crossed the road and kneeled behind the truck and watched him. As he crouched to insert a new clip, Melko gripped his arm, not in anger or even haste, and said: 'Don't fire again till the gas comes.'

For a moment their eyes met, then Chuck looked away, to his left, at the end of the road where, above a tall black mass of pines, a glowing cloud hid the moon.

It took five silent minutes for the truck to come, then Visconti had the tear gas, squatting beside Chuck who stood isolated within the percussion and flash of each round, aware of nothing save the kick of the rifle against his shoulder and cheek bone, the smell of powder, the dark rectangles of the windows and what he sensed behind them. When the clip pinged out and clattered against the

fender he reloaded, half-crouched yet exposed over the hood, his
eyes on the windows where Phil, surprised by the gas, had filled his
lungs with a hot burning solid which he immediately recognized; he
expelled it, then dropping the rifle he held his nose and mouth. His
lungs were empty. He stood up, his flesh and tightly closed eyes
burning; he waved an arm toward the window and the men behind
the truck, and was about to flee out of the room and into the air
when Chuck, standing erectly now, fired his last clip, hearing at
some time Melko yelling 'Cease fire! Cease fire!' He did not know
how many rounds he fired after that: perhaps four, perhaps three.
Then Melko grabbed his shoulder and rifle and spun him around,
both of them exposed to the acrid-smelling windows, as if already
they knew the firing was over.

'Goddammit, Sergeant! We had him! We had him!'

NEXT MORNING after chow he offered to clean Visconti's rifle;
but Visconti, with the awe of a bat boy, said he would clean
it himself. Late the following afternoon the Corporal of the Guard
showed him the Oak Harbor paper; he glanced at his picture,
grunted, and went outside to the blacktop parade field, where a
corporal was drilling troops. The day was hazy, with a faint glare
from the covered sun. For nearly an hour he stood smoking, field-
stripping the butts, and watching the troops in pressed green
utilities marching back and forth and in squared turns, their rifles
slanted upward in perfect angles, their boot heels clomping in uni-
son. Then he went back inside. By Taps that night he had picked
up six newspapers: one on the deck in the head, four on bunks in
squad bays, and one under the pool table in the rec room. The ones
in the head and rec room were easiest, for each room was empty.
He stalked the other four, waiting until a squad bay was either
empty (this happened twice) or until no one was around the bunk
that held it, and he could stand with his back to the scattered troops
and slip the paper under his shirt.

The other two sergeants were married, so he shared his room
with no one. That night, while outside his closed door the barracks
grew quiet, he lay on his bunk and read the story and studied his
picture: a full length profile, his right side to the camera, his cap
restored to his head, his right arm down at his side, holding the

rifle. On the second page were small pictures of the Korsmeyers, only their faces. The picture of Korsmeyer distorted Chuck's memory of the other face: drained white, turned in frozen anguish to one side, averting its open eyes from the holes in its chest and throat. To recall clearly the man who had tried to stab his wife and who had shot at him with a .22, Chuck turned back to the first page, to his own picture, where he stood forever poised in peaceful silence.

But that night's silence stayed with him and changed to something else, as if he had taken restful leave of a woman's bed, only to fall unwillingly into months of continence. It stayed with him through the long summer, broken by nights with Toni; it stayed with him through the fall when, on the eve of her husband's return, Toni told him goodbye with ceremonial lust and sorrow, Chuck feigning both and leaving her house long before dawn. In the dull rains of winter he returned often to the newspapers; they were faded yellow as in sickness, dry and delicate in his fingers, and he handled them like butterfly wings, fearing for their lives.

Andromache

PETE AND BECKY stayed up with her that night, until she thought she could sleep; then Pete went home and Becky slept with her. But Ellen woke three hours later when the couple next door returned from the New Year's Eve party at the Officers' Club. She heard car doors slamming and women's high laughter—there seemed to be two couples—then a man singing. She reached out, and her hand touched Becky's breast; she withdrew it and lay awake for the rest of the night. She thought of Posy, nine years old now, and perhaps in twenty years or even less she would go through this too. She thought of Ronnie, fatherless at five, and already so much like his father; but Ronnie wouldn't have to bear this: he was a man, so he would merely die. And she thought of Joe trying to reach the escape hatch as the plane dived faster toward earth.

They found Joe's body, but she never saw it, and the funeral was with closed caskets. Ellen sat erectly between Posy and Ronnie. She did not cry, though her mother and Joe's mother did: subdued but continual sobbing, while the two older men sat quietly, their faces transfixed in bewildered grief. Posy didn't cry, either. Ronnie sniffled once but Ellen whispered in his ear: *Be a strong Marine;* and he bit his lip and stared at Joe's casket, flanked by the caskets of the pilot and the crewman.

At the funeral Ellen learned that the enlist crewman, a petty officer, had been only twenty-four years old; so next day she called a friend at Navy Relief, asking her to check on his widow. He probably didn't have much insurance, Ellen said, and she may need money to get home. Then Ellen drove south with her parents, to Sacramento.

She found an apartment near a school for Posy, and started

taking courses in shorthand and typing. She didn't try to make friends. Some nights she had a drink with a couple across the hall. They were in their late twenties, and they bored her. Gradually she realized that she was boring them too: her talk was of the Marine Corps—the Fleet Marine Force bases and travel and funny anecdotes—a world as alien to this odd flabby couple as theirs was to her.

On most nights she stayed in the apartment and watched television or read magazines. Or, when Posy and Ronnie were asleep, she looked at the photographs in her album or projected home movies on a portable screen. The pictures were painful, but she was glad she had taken them. For sometimes she could not remember Joe's face. His image often appeared in her mind but when she concentrated on it, tried to keep it there, it began to fade. Then she would look at a picture. If she were out of the apartment, she turned to one in her billfold. In that one he was wearing his green uniform and major's oak leaves. At home, she would hurry to the bedroom where an eight-by-ten colored photograph was on the dressing table: he wore blues and captain's bars. She had no pictures of Joe in civilian clothes, except in the movies.

It took her four months to look at the movie she had taken on Christmas Day: Ronnie and Posy with their presents and Joe sipping coffee and smiling and lighting a pipe; then he was running beside Ronnie, holding the bicycle seat, and three times she reversed the film and watched the moment when he released the bicycle and she had focused on his face as he called softly: *keep steering, Son, keep steering*—She began to cry, but she watched the rest: the sandwiches and cookies and punch bowl, the living room and Joe in his blues, and her clean kitchen.

She remembered an uncle's funeral when she was fifteen. His widow had spent almost an entire day at the funeral home, where his dead face was there to look at; it wasn't his real face, it was younger than Ellen had ever seen it, but it was dead. A woman could look at it, speak to it, touch it. But *she* couldn't. Her memories of Joe were alive: he was talking, he was smiling at her, he was stern, he was walking on the cold beach at Whidbey Island, or kissing her and going to the plane.

She went to the kitchen and made an Old Fashioned, then sat in the living room again, staring at the white movie screen. She wanted to talk, but not to the couple across the hall, or to the young girls in the business school, or to her mother. For she was thinking about Camp Pendleton and Marine wives: *Remember during Korea how we'd read two papers every day, the morning and evening ones, and we'd be waiting for the mail as soon as we woke up in the morning, that was almost the first thing you thought about—except sometimes you woke up, mostly on Sundays when there's no mail, and you'd lie there thinking it'll always be like this: alone in the morning—but most days it was mail you thought about and you'd try to forget it because the postman wouldn't come until ten and about nine-fifteen or so you could see women opening their front doors and looking in the mailbox, sometimes even sticking a hand in it, then they'd look up and down the street. They'd have brooms or mops in their hands. They knew the mail hadn't come yet but they couldn't help looking—Oh, I was the same. Remember how it was? How terrible? But we made it, didn't we. We by God made it—*

The next day she wrote to Colonel James Harkness at Camp Pendleton, California. He answered within a week: he had taken action on her request, he wrote, and he could assure her that a position with Navy Relief would always be open for her. If she would notify him several weeks prior to her arrival, he would find quarters in Oceanside. He and Marcia looked forward to seeing her again, and the Corps had lost one of its finest officers.

She replied that she would be there in June, then she took the children to her mother's and told them she wanted to see Pete and Becky again before moving to Oceanside. As she told them this, she looked at Posy and wanted to say: *I'll send you to college in the midwest, far away from the Corps, and you can marry a man like that one across the hall, a man who—who what? A man you can live with.* But she said: 'We'll do a lot of swimming there.'

Then she flew to Seattle. Pete and Becky met her at the airport; she sat between them in the car, and from Seattle to Deception Pass they talked about Whidbey Island friends and the weather. The sky was grey and the air damp and chilling. But when they approached Deception Pass, Ellen was silent. They rounded a curve and she looked at the grey roiling water and, across it, at the evergreens of Whidbey Island, and her heart quickened. She saw the rapids under the bridge, then they were on it: high above the Pass, and ahead of them were dark tall trees, and a winding blacktop road and, trembling, she lit a cigarette. Becky took her hand. As they left the bridge and entered the trees, Ellen said: 'Pete, would you take me to the salvage area tomorrow?'

'Sure.'

'I want to see the plane. I never saw Joe, or the plane either. Did they bring it here?'

Pete said yes, they had; and Becky squeezed her hand.

Two days before Christmas, nine days before his death, Joe Forrest had come home in the evening while Ellen was in the kitchen, making pastries. He looked at them for a while, pausing over each tray as if he were inspecting the enlisted mess, tasted a couple of them, then said gently: 'Make big cookies. The troops like big cookies.'

'Oh, Joe,' she said, 'do you really think I have to? What'll we do with these?'

'We'll eat them,' he said, and mixed her a martini.

He went to the bedroom to take off his uniform, and she thought of him going through the ritual, carefully hanging the trousers and shirt on a wooden hangar, the blouse on another. Then he would spitshine the shoes, cordovans so heavily coated with polish now that his daily shining took hardly any time at all. He would finish by polishing the brass buckle and tip of his web belt, putting on a sport shirt and slacks, and then he would mix their second drinks. But she didn't wait for it. While he was still in the bedroom she called that she was going to Becky's for a minute and a roast was in the oven, but she'd be back before it was done.

Walking to Becky's, she looked through the windows of the officers' houses, all of them alike: picture windows and fireplaces and car ports, and cords of wood stacked outside. Though it wasn't six o'clock yet, the sky had been black for an hour. The wind was cold and damp, and she shivered. She always told Joe that she loved Whidbey Island and she told the officers' wives too; but she was from California and she hated the island and Puget Sound which enclosed it. She was certain that Joe felt the same, but he had been a Marine for too long and was cheerfully resigned to discomfort. She turned up the Crawfords' sidewalk, hurrying, her overcoat useless against the wind. Becky answered the door with a drink in her hand; they went to the living room, and Pete stood up.

'Where's the old man?' he said.

'Shining his shoes and drinking. What else do Marines do before dinner?'

Pete had been an ace in the Second World War and he was now a squadron commander. Ellen looked condescendingly at his uniform: he was wearing two-thirds of his Navy blues, having taken off his coat and tie and rolled up the sleeves of his white shirt.

'Those pastries I spent all afternoon on,' she said to Becky. 'The Major has just disapproved them.'

'He *did*?'

Becky smiled, and her face wrinkled. She was a tall woman with bleached hair and a face that was lined and tan. She played golf nearly every day, even at Whidbey Island; she had said only snow could keep her away from golf, and if it ever snowed she might even paint the balls red and play in that.

'Make big cookies,' Ellen said. 'The troops like big cookies.'

Pete brought Ellen a Scotch and water, then put another log on the fire.

'He'll probably tell me to make hot dogs too,' she said.

Pete was smiling at her.

'What are they drinking?' he said.

'Joe's making that rum punch.'

'Drunk Marines in Officers' Country. You stay in the house, Becky.'

'Maybe I won't. Who was that snappy one at the main gate today? About five o'clock.'

'Langley,' Ellen said.

She knew them all. Joe had their photographs on the bulkhead in his office and each time a new man reported in, he brought the photograph home and showed it to her. When he had brought Langley's picture home she had studied it for a long while, speaking his name aloud, and thinking of *lanky*, because Joe said he was. A week later he was a gate sentry and as Ellen stopped the car she had rolled her window down; when he saluted she had smiled and said: *Good afternoon, Langley.* He had never seen her before, but he knew the Major's car, and for a moment after his salute they had grinned at each other, proudly.

'He's darling,' Becky said.

The fresh log was burning now and its warmth reached Ellen's face.

'He didn't salute when I drove through,' Pete said.

'He didn't?' Ellen said. 'Did you tell Joe?'

'Oh, he's teasing. It was the sharpest salute he's had in weeks.'

'They're *all* sharp,' Pete said. 'I wish the Navy was like that.'

Becky brought an ash tray to Ellen. As she leaned over to place it on the arm of the chair, Ellen looked closely at her face. Then she glanced at Pete, who was talking about the old Navy when sailors had discipline. She was thinking that pilots' wives were a little better off—in the matter of aging anyway. Becky looked a year or two older than Pete, but at least they both appeared near middle-age. Perhaps because of jet-flying, pilots aged nearly as quickly as their wives.

But not infantry officers: during peacetime Joe's work was almost relaxing, or Ellen thought so. He was outdoors more often than not—hiking, climbing hills, running—and his trouser size had increased only one inch since their wedding, while she had gone from size ten to twelve. Even at Whidbey Island, where he commanded a security barracks and his troops did little more than stand guard, Joe exercised daily: handball or running at noon. During his tours of infantry duty he went to the field for days or weeks and came back looking relaxed and sunburned, to tell her funny stories: a lieutenant who got lost, a king snake in the chaplain's sleeping bag . . .

To occupy herself during their separations, and also because it was expected of her, she was active in wives' clubs. At Whidbey Island she was their president, a good one and proud of it; she felt that she was like Joe: the senior Marine at a Naval air station, and she had impressed the rival service. At the Armed Forces Day cocktail party, she had invited the Admiral's wife to go riding with her. *But it won't be much of a ride*, she had said, *because all the horses are nags.* Then she had talked about that for ten minutes. Three weeks later there was a new petty officer in charge of the stables and the

Admiral had appointed a full commander to buy horses. Through the Special Services Officer, Ellen had arranged for a ladies' night at the hobby shop on Tuesdays and the indoor swimming pool, which had been used solely for water survival training, on Thursdays, so that wives of deployed pilots could make pottery, and swim. She felt a special pity for pilots' wives. Their husbands were gone for seven months each year, flying from carriers in the Western Pacific. They flew A3D's and it was rare when a year passed without at least one wife attending a corpseless memorial service.

Flames from the big log were reaching the chimney now, and Ellen leaned back in her chair, moving her face from the heat. Her legs were comfortably hot. Pete rose to mix another drink, but Ellen told him she had to leave.

'I've had a break,' she said. 'Now I can go back and be a Marine again.'

By the time she reached the sidewalk in front of the Crawfords' house, she was cold. The wind was stronger and she blinked and wiped her eyes. Across the island, on the west side, she could hear A3D's taking off and climbing into the wet black sky.

The next day, Christmas Eve, Ellen baked large cookies. She also stuffed and roasted their turkey, for she was having Christmas dinner that night, so it wouldn't interfere with the open house. Pete and Becky were coming to dinner.

She didn't mind the work. Having the open house was her idea, because they had never had one for Joe's troops, at any duty station, and she told him this was their last chance. He would be a lieutenant-colonel soon, his next command a battalion. Then, except for a few Staff NCOs and clerks at battalion headquarters, she wouldn't know the names and faces of his troops anymore. So she had planned the Christmas open house, and Joe had placed a handwritten invitation on the bulletin board at the barracks. He had told his Staff NCOs and two officers that no Marine would be forced to attend.

Christmas Eve morning, Ellen was up at five. Hers was the only lighted house among the officers' quarters; from her living room window she could see the red light of the radar tower at the Seaplane Base; out her kitchen window, which faced the water, there was only darkness. She was outside in the cold fog getting kindling and two logs when she heard six-thirty reveille being sounded for the sailors in the squadrons' barracks a mile away. By the time her neighbors' lights went on, she was giddy from coffee and cigarettes on an empty stomach, the kitchen and living room smelled of freshly-baked cookies and wood smoke, and one countertop was filled with platters of cookies. Shortly after eight o'clock, she looked out the kitchen window at the grey choppy water and a crash boat moving slowly through the fog, clearing the seaplane lanes of driftwood; by then she had baked three hundred and fifty cookies.

She was only beginning. Posy helped her and they were in the kitchen all day, making sandwiches and stuffing the turkey. The fog never lifted and Posy kept adding wood to the fire. At four o'clock there were three hundred sandwiches and a thousand cookies; then Ellen put the turkey in the oven and Posy delivered platters of sandwiches to twelve neighbors who would store them in refrigerators. Just before Joe came home, Ellen made up her face and combed her hair; when he entered the house, unbuttoning his green raincoat, she said:

'You'd better get some more rum.'

'There's plenty.'

'You know these Marines, Joe.'

He started to object, but then he smiled and said all right, and went out into the fog again.

The Crawfords arrived for dinner at eight, and they drank with Joe in the living room, the three of them gathered at the fireplace, while Ellen had her drink in the kitchen. Becky offered to help but Ellen said no, it was all done and there wasn't room for two in the kitchen anyway. She put her drink down among the dishes on the countertop and then forgot it; when she noticed it again, Joe was mixing second drinks for the Crawfords and himself and she gave him her glass and told him to stiffen it. Once she had two cigarettes burning in different ash trays.

She lighted two candles on the table and said: Let's eat the bird. They filed past the counter separating kitchen from dinette and served themselves turkey and dressing, peas and creamed cauliflower, rolls and jello salad. Joe went around the table, pouring the first glasses of wine; he gave wine to Posy and Ronnie too. Ellen served herself last and sat down. Then she found that she wasn't hungry. All day she had nibbled, eating cookies and small sandwiches as unconsciously as she had lighted thirty or more cigarettes. For the past hour she had tasted the dinner. So she took only a few bites of everything and drank a lot of wine and before dessert she was tight: not cheerfully, though, but tired and foggy. She drank three cups of coffee while Joe and the Crawfords started on the second bottle of wine and their voices grew louder. Then Joe was telling her that he would fly to southern California next week, to buy uniforms from the tailor shop at Camp Pendleton.

'Who's flying you?' she said.

'Larry Sievers. In an A3D.'

'Why one of *those*? They won't let you aboard anyway, will they?'

'We'll run him through the pressure chamber,' Pete said.

'Oh. Why don't you just go down on a prop plane?'

'I've never been in one of the big birds before.'

There was no argument to that. It had been his reason too often: for going to a three week Army Jungle Warfare school, returning to tell her of eating monkeys; going to a mountain leadership course in the Sierras, where he learned to rapelle from cliffs; and, also in the Sierras, a survival school where he was interrogated and thrown into a cold mountain stream and kept for hours in a wooden box and finally was left in the field for three days with only a knife and no food.

'Well, if you're going down where all the sunshine is, you'd better bring me a nice present. I rate it—' she looked at Becky '—since you're making me a pilot's wife. Pilots always bring back nice things from their deployments.'

The lines deepened and spread in Becky's face as she smiled at Ellen. But Ellen looked down, into her coffee cup, then she drained it and poured herself a glass of wine. She was remembering an afternoon last winter when Pete had been deployed on a carrier; there was a light, cold rain, blown almost horizontally from the sea. Driving past the golf course, Ellen had seen a solitary player, clothed in what appeared to be a wool jacket and ski pants and, over them, a hooded plastic suit. Then she recognized Becky and sounded the horn and Becky turned: the golf bag hanging from one shoulder—the earth was too soaked for carts—an iron in her left hand, and the right arm lifted in a cheerful wave.

'Joe, don't we have some brandy?'

'Sure. Becky? Pete?'

The men took their brandy to the living room. Posy and Becky cleared the table and scraped plates, while Ellen put Ronnie to bed.

'I want to put up the tree,' he said when she had him covered.

'You had three glasses of wine, corporal. You'd be drunk on duty.'

When she got back to the kitchen, Posy had filled the dishwasher and turned it on.

'The pots wouldn't go in,' she said.

Ellen kissed her.

'Thank you, baby. We can do them while Daddy puts up the tree.'

She took her brandy to the living room, where Pete was standing with his back to the fire and saying: 'We had a good summer last year, but I missed it: I had the duty that day.'

Ellen chuckled. It was an old island joke, but like all good jokes it was true and you either had to laugh or curse. She was feeling better now that her work was nearly done, and she was going to tease Joe again about his three day deployment to California; but with her mouth open to speak, she looked at Becky and said:

'It's good brandy.'

You could never tell. Navy wives often talked of deployments, but Becky rarely did. Ellen recalled a wives' bridge party at the Officers' Club at Camp Pendleton during the Korean War: at one table a major's wife was talking loudly about the Chosin Reservoir. *They're cut off and outnumbered*, she had said, *but by God you wait and see. They'll make it to the beach.* Until finally a young girl, probably a lieutenant's wife, threw down her cards and rose suddenly, her chair overturning, and cried: *Shut up! Shut up, you hard-nosed bitch!* She had left the Club then, walking quickly past the quiet staring tables of foursomes. Ellen had tried to catch up with her in the parking lot, but she hurried away: an unknown girl whom Ellen never saw again and never forgot.

Deployments weren't that bad, no one was being shot at, but you couldn't really tell what was bad. When Joe returned from Korea, Ellen had thought if he could finish his career without ever going to war again, she could bear anything. But three years ago he had gone to Okinawa with an infantry battalion for thirteen months and, after a while, that separation was no better than the first. Again, though her mother invited her to Sacramento, she had stayed at Camp Pendleton with the other battalion wives. They did Navy Relief work, interviewing Marines who needed money, recommending loans or grants. At bridge tables their conversations finally came to sex; sometimes they jokingly alluded to their husbands' probable infidelities, but they grinned with only their lips. Once at a luncheon a captain's wife finished her second martini then looked around the table and said *God*DAMN, *I'm horny*, and they all laughed, their raised glasses tilting and dripping.

Maybe it didn't really matter whether your husband was being shot at, or was flying jet bombers in peacetime, or was merely being tempted by Okinawan whores. Maybe, at the heart of it, it was simply that he was gone; and when a man is gone he might not come back. Even when he does, nothing can replenish the four hundred days you spent without him. So, glancing at Becky, she did not mention planes or separations.

When the Crawfords left they all stood under the mistletoe and kissed. Joe put his arm around her waist, and she drew in her stomach muscles, and they stood in the open doorway until the Crawfords had walked out of sight. Ellen shivered. Joe closed the door, then put a log on the fire and went to the kitchen to mix Old Fashioneds. Ellen went to the bedroom for her diaphragm. The children were asleep; she went to the couch in the living room, and waited for Joe.

BY CHRISTMAS morning the fog was gone. They were awake at six, bringing Posy and Ronnie to the living room where the gifts were laid out. Posy no longer believed in Santa Claus but, for Ronnie, she pretended; while he was trying to play with all his toys at once, she quietly kissed Joe and Ellen. At precisely seven o'clock, as she had planned, Ellen served breakfast.

All morning the sky was grey. The water was grey too, and choppy, and the visible portion of beach was covered with grey and brown driftwood. At mid-morning Posy went to the neighbors' and brought back the sandwiches. Joe was outside with Ronnie, teaching him to ride his new bicycle. Ellen had thought he was too young, but Joe said there were five-year-old kids riding bikes all over the neighborhood. When Posy came back with the twelfth and last platter of sandwiches, Ellen took the movie camera outside. She told Posy to come get in the pictures but Posy, whose face was red and eyes watering, wanted to stay by the fire.

From a distance of perhaps a hundred feet, Ellen focused on Joe and Ronnie: they were approaching her, Joe running alongside the bicycle, holding the seat. Then he let go. Ellen got that in the picture too: held the camera on him as he called softly: Keep steering, Son, keep steering—

She turned quickly to Ronnie. The front wheel was veering from left to right, his pedalling was slowing, and finally the bicycle leaned to one side and he went with it: falling on his shoulder, lying for only an instant on the hard earth, the dead grass, then rising again. Ellen moved in for a close-up of his face: hurt and determined, he looked at the camera as if he were about to curse, then he turned away and, grabbing the handlebars, jerked the bicycle upright. Ellen went back into the house. By noon, Ronnie was beginning to ride.

The open house was to begin at two o'clock. At one-thirty Joe put on his blues and she fastened the high collar for him and, with masking tape, removed lint from his blouse. She changed clothes, then took moving pictures of the table: silver punch bowl and silver platters of sandwiches and cookies. She swung the camera toward the living room, pausing on the fireplace, the hors d'oeuvres on the coffee table, and Joe, who was sitting in his easy chair. She went to the kitchen and, smiling at herself, focused the camera on the clean stove, bare of pots; the empty sink; the countertops which she had cleared and sponged; and the deck. Then she went to the living room and waited.

She didn't wait long. At exactly two o'clock Captain Jack Flaherty arrived, wearing a suit and tie. He was a bachelor. Then Lieutenant Ed Williams came, with his wife Katie. He was slim and boyish and wore civilian clothes; he looked afraid when he saw Joe in blues. Then he came into the living room and saw Jack in the dark suit and tie, and his relief was so apparent that Ellen almost laughed aloud. Katie was a pretty brunette with rather dark skin and faintly rouged cheeks; she began talking as soon as she entered the front door, but by the time she was settled on the couch with a glass of punch, she was quiet. Ed had done more preparation: he didn't run out of conversation until at least five minutes had gone by. Then he was finished. He looked around the room and said, very quietly to Katie, that it was a nice house. She nodded and asked for a cigarette. They had a friendly low-voiced argument about who was smoking more. Then Katie noticed that the others were listening and she blushed and said: 'He smokes more than I do.'

'He drinks more too,' Ellen said. 'He needs a refill.'

She got up and took his glass to the punch bowl. Then First Sergeant Rosener came, with Paula; they had been in for twenty-one years and they talked. So did Gunnery Sergeant Holmes, who got there shortly before three; his wife had divorced him two years ago, when he was ordered to Whidbey Island, because she refused to go with him. She was tired moving, she said, and she stayed in San Diego. Or that is the way he told it. Holmes and First Sergeant Rosener were wearing green winter uniforms; Jack and Ed seemed embarrassed by that.

So with the arrival of the Staff NCOs, there was conversation: five men talking shop, and Ellen and Paula joined them whenever they could. Ellen called Rosener and Holmes First Sergeant and Gunny; she addressed the officers by their first names. All the men called her ma'am, and Paula and Katie called her Ellen, but Katie was uncomfortable about it. Then at three o'clock Ellen began waiting again. At three-thirty she and Ed Williams looked simultaneously at their watches. Ed and Gunny Holmes exchanged frowns. Ellen waited another fifteen minutes, listening beneath the conversation for a knock at the front door, then she excused herself and went to the kitchen. She stared through the window. Their back yard sloped down to the beach: dead grass, then dirty sand littered with driftwood. She clasped her hands together as in prayer, squeezing until her fingers reddened. From the living room she could hear Gunny Holmes' voice above the others: 'Does the Major know Colonel 'Cold Steel' Harkness?'

'*Very* well. I was his S-3 on my last tour.'

'I was in his battalion in the Fifth Marines. In fifty-six. I see in the *Gazette* where he's made bird colonel.'

'Now *that's* a Marine officer,' the First Sergeant said—

But Ellen didn't hear the rest. She didn't hear anything distinctly now, only the sound of their voices, for at that moment a dark grey seaplane appeared to her left, descending toward the water. Her first reaction was anger: the plane had probably been on patrol since morning and, now that Christmas was over, the men were coming home. In the enlisted quonset huts and officers' houses, women had been alone all day; watching the children with their toys, taking pictures, receiving phone calls from home. The plane smoothly struck the water and moved westward, toward the Seaplane base, and now Ed Williams was talking:'—dropped four points all the way, then he got to three hundred rapid and put on the wrong dope, and got seven maggies and three deuces—' then laughter, and First Sergeant Rosener now, starting another story about rifle ranges. Watching the seaplane, she clasped her hands and squeezed until the fingers reddened. Then she looked at the table in the dinette, at the stacked cookies and sandwiches, and thought of the troops: some would be in the barracks, lying on bunks and talking about women or what they would do when they got out of the Corps; others would be in bars, playing bowling machines: losers buy the beer. *They should be bachelors*, she thought. *They should all*—Then she had to raise her hands to her face and quickly wipe her eyes.

She was going to the punch bowl when she heard a knock on the front door. She turned quickly, immediately angered by her speed and the leap of hope in her breast. Before going to the door, she paused to fill her glass and light a cigarette. But when she opened the door, she looked over the shoulders of the lone Marine standing there and scanned the front lawn and the street before the house. Then she looked at him. It was Anderson, and for an instant she thought of slamming the door and leaving him to stand there, cold and puzzled, before returning to the barracks to tell the others.

He was a tall nineteen year old boy with a round, pleading face which was now smiling at her. The width of his belly and hips was more than even an old officer or Staff NCO could bear with any sort of pride. He had his own car, he received money from home, and he was the only private in the barracks. Joe was thinking of giving him an Undesirable Discharge, because of repeated minor offenses. Ellen smiled.

'Merry Christmas, Anderson. I'm glad you could come.'

In spite of herself, she nearly was. For she spent the next hour controlling her face and voice, adding to the conversation, smiling and nodding and passing platters and filling glasses, knowing that no one else was coming.

Captain Flaherty was the first to leave. Anderson left when the First Sergeant and Paula did; Ellen watched him from the door, walking on the First Sergeant's left, nodding his head and laughing. Then Gunny Holmes glanced at Ed, who nodded, and all three of them stood at once. At the door Ellen told Katie to drop by some time. She didn't watch them walk to their cars; she firmly closed the door, and went to the living room, where Joe was looking out the window and biting his pipestem.

'I wish Ed wouldn't do that,' he said.

Ellen went to the window. On the sidewalk Ed and Gunny Holmes were talking angrily.

'Is Holmes arguing?' she said.

'Agreeing. Ed's probably telling him he wants a piece of the Staff NCOs tomorrow. The ones that didn't come.'

'Good for him.'

Joe flushed, but she didn't care.

'And Holmes will probably take the troops to the drill field tomorrow and chew them out,' Joe said. 'Then he'll harass them for a few days.'

'I hope he does.'

He flushed again and started to say something, but instead he knocked the ashes from his pipe.

'Bad for morale,' he said.

'*Morale*. Oh, Joe—Joe, *look* at that food!'

She pointed at the table, where sandwiches and cookies were piled. Only the punch bowl was nearly empty.

'And there's more in the kitchen. They don't even *care* about you. You bring their problems home at night, you get them out of jail and make them write to their mothers and you patch up their marriages. You even work out their *budg*ets and you don't do that in your own home—'

He interrupted her. He only said her name, very quietly, but his face was stern.

'I know,' she said. 'I'm not complaining, but they don't *care*, Joe. You give them everything and they don't care if you're even alive.'

'They probably don't, during peacetime. But that doesn't matter. It's combat that counts, and when the shooting starts they look for a leader. Even Rosener and Holmes would. I remember—' He paused, staring into the fire place, and when he spoke again his voice was impassioned with memory '—when I took over that company in Korea, it was up on the lines. There weren't any platoon leaders left and the exec was running the show. I don't think he even had a year in the Corps and he was so confused that he got tied down to the CP, looking at maps and talking to battalion on the radio. I got there about noon—'

She turned her back and went to the punch bowl, then past it, to the kitchen where the bourbon was. He followed her.

'Are you listening?'

'Yes.'

'Here: I'll make you an Old Fashioned. Anyway, I wanted to get oriented, so I crawled up to the perimeter—' He went to the sink, looking out the window. '—I went to different foxholes, checking out the terrain with binoculars, and pretty soon I could feel the effect I was having, and I stopped crawling. They hadn't seen an officer for a day or so, I guess. I walked up and down the line and stopped at each hole and chatted with the men—' He chuckled, and gave her the drink. '—pretty soon I drew some incoming, but it didn't matter: they knew where we were anyway.'

'I wish they could need you without getting shot at.'

'Oh, there's more to it than that. Most of them didn't come because they'd be uncomfortable or because it would look like brown-nosing.'

'Like Anderson.'

Joe smiled.

'He came for an Honorable Discharge. But he won't get it. The others came because they're professionals.'

'I should have known it would be that way.'

'I should have warned you.'

'No: I should have known.'

She called Posy, who had been watching television in a bedroom. Ronnie was playing at a friend's house.

'Would you like to have some friends over tomorrow?' Ellen said. 'You'll have plenty of refreshments.'

She waved toward the sandwiches and cookies on the table. Posy watched her quietly.

'But there's still enough for eighty hungry Marines, so let's give most of it to the neighbors.'

Joe kissed her cheek and hugged her, then went to the bedroom. Posy covered a platter of sandwiches with waxed paper, and took it outside. When Joe came to the kitchen, wearing a sport shirt and slacks, Ellen asked him to make an Old Fashioned. He touched her shoulder.

'I'm sorry,' he said.

'Don't worry about it. I just to have to figure out what to do.'

'Looks like Posy's taking care of it.'

'That's not what I mean.'

'What *do* you mean?'

'I don't know yet.'

During the short dusk and the beginning of night, Posy delivered all but a hundred cookies and twenty sandwiches. Sometimes Ellen stood at the living room window and watched her: a platter held in both arms, walking straight-backed under the streetlights. When she had finished, she called friends and asked them to come over the next afternoon. Once Ellen heard her say: We have a few left-overs from this big open house Mother had. Ellen brought her a glass of sherry.

'It'll make your feet warm,' she said.

At nine o'clock, when she was kissing Posy goodnight, the phone rang. Joe answered. Ellen went to Ronnie's bedroom and pulled the blankets over his shoulders. Near his face on the pillow was a half-eaten oatmeal cookie. She dropped it in the wastebasket. In the hall, Joe was chuckling into the phone.

'Okay, boy,' he said. 'Then we can get a battalion from Lejeune and occupy.'

He laughed again. Ellen was putting on her coat and scarf when he hung up.

'I'm going to Becky's for a minute. Who was that?'

'Larry Sievers. He says we'll steal that A3D next week and bomb Castro.'

'Where's he drinking tonight?'

'At home.'

'That's nice, for a change.'

She stepped outside. The wind was strong and, walking against it, she turned her face and clenched her hands in her pockets. She hadn't told Joe goodbye, and that bothered her. When she got to Becky's she knocked fast and loud, her back to the wind.

'A flop,' she said, when Becky opened the door.

She had three drinks. With the first one she was still controlling herself, telling them very calmly why no one had come. After the second she was complaining bitterly, and she knew it, but she couldn't stop.

'Goddamnit,' she said to Becky, when she was finally ready to leave, 'we don't have ranks and service numbers. We're *women*.'

'Bless you for that,' Pete said, and he put his arm around her waist as they walked to the door. She forgot to draw in her stomach muscles.

'A lot of good it does,' she said, and kissed them both and left. The wind struck her back now, pushing her forward.

Joe was asleep in his chair in the living room, an open book on his lap; the fire was dying. She poked the coals and put another log on the andirons. Then in their bedroom she undressed and put on a silk kimono. Joe had brought it from Japan and once, when she was wearing it over her naked body as she was now, he had reached inside the wide arm and touched her breast. She had wondered how he learned that. At the mirror she combed her hair and freshened her lipstick and dabbed perfume on her wrists and throat. Then she was ready. She did not even look at the drawer where her diaphragm was. She walked past it, and into the living room where she turned off the lamps and arranged throw-pillows on the carpet before the fire. With the cover flap, she marked Joe's place in the book, *Russia and the West Under Lenin and Stalin*, and set it on the coffee table. Then she started waking him up. He was annoyed at first, but soon she was taking care of that.

AT THE DINNER table two days after Christmas, Joe told her about the pressure chamber. They had simulated forty thousand feet and taught him to use an oxygen mask. They also taught him to bail out. There were three seats in an A3D, he told her, two facing forward and one aft. The escape hatch was opposite the seat facing aft; it opened onto a chute in the belly of the plane. A horizontal bar was at the top of the hatch and you had to grab it with your arms crossed and pull yourself into the chute. Ellen watched him across the table as he held up his arms, the forearms crossed and the hands grasping an imaginary bar. Then he stood up to show how his body would turn as he uncrossed his arms, and he would slide out of the plane on his belly.

'There's not much time,' he said. 'Everybody's got to move out fast.'

But no one did. She told him goodbye four days before New Year's and he said he'd be back for the party. On New Year's Eve they flew back from California and, minutes away from Whidbey Island, they went down.

When her doorbell rang in mid-afternoon Ellen was in the bedroom checking her social calendar. She found the date of the wives' club luncheon in December; that was when her last period had begun. Then she counted days on the calendar, until her finger touched Christmas. She counted them again, and decided she had probably not conceived. Now she wasn't sure whether she wanted to or not. *It's up to you*, Joe had said Christmas night and a couple of times since then. But she was thirty-five and she had gained weight and maybe a pregnancy would ruin her figure forever. When the child was five, she would be forty; fifteen, fifty; twenty, fifty-five. That was all right. But her weight.... And if Joe got orders in June she would be—she counted on her fingers—six months pregnant and travelling perhaps across the country: motels and those weary distorted days of emptying one house and filling another: packing boxes and wardrobes and scratched furniture and confusion.

But she was thirty-five. She'd be forty soon, and she had two

children (*a boy and a girl*, people said, *such nice planning*) and she was
the president of the wives' club and she was the Major's wife.
Gunny Holmes might have marched the troops to the drill field and
chewed them out, but it wouldn't have been for her and even if he
had mentioned her name, it wouldn't have mattered to them. Ed
Williams might have admonished the Staff NCOs about courtesy
and loyalty to the Commanding Officer. No one, though, would be
told: *You hurt Mrs. Forrest.* There was no recourse, either. She
couldn't scowl at the Marines as they saluted her at the gates; they
would only smile at her and joke about it in the barracks. There was
nothing, nothing at all, and she was again counting the calendar
days since the last wives' club luncheon when the doorbell rang.

She waited for Posy to answer it, but heard nothing; then she
rose, still trying to decide, wishing it were already decided for her,
that she had already conceived, but size twelve, she'd have to diet
and exercise. . . . Going through the living room she saw Posy out
the back window, getting two logs from the wood pile, and as her
hand went to the doorknob she glimpsed the dying fire: *sweet sweet
Posy.* Then she opened the door and Pete was standing there, his
white cap in his hand—that was the first thing she noticed—and the
collar of his blue topcoat turned up: six feet of somber dark blue and
beyond his anguished face and bare head was the grey sky. Her
hand tightened on the doorknob and she opened her mouth to speak
but couldn't, silenced by a welling urge to be suspended here
forever, to be deceived and comforted and never to know anything
at all. But he was looking at his cap, then at her, and a hand went
up and through his hair, and he said: 'Ellen. Ellen, baby—'

And stopped again. She saw fire, explosions, a parachute failing
to open and someone unreal—it wasn't Joe, it *wasn't*—falling down
and down without cease, as in a dream. Then she was underwater
and a plane was sinking past her, descending slowly and without
hope, and she had to get to it and open it somehow but she couldn't
breathe—

'Is it Joe?' she said.

He nodded and stepped forward but before he could touch her
she said: 'In the water?'

He said: 'No, Olympic Peninsula,' then grabbed her as she fell toward him; she gave all her weight to his locked arms and pressed her face against his coarse Navy topcoat, not breathing; then finally she did: a deep dry audible breath, and she said: 'He didn't get out?'

She felt his head shaking against her own, heard him whisper: 'Nobody did,' and as if on some strangely distant part of her body she felt his hand patting her back, and she suddenly knew she hadn't conceived, it could never work out that way, nothing ever could, he was gone and she would have a period soon, her womb's dark red weeping. How could he be gone? It was the last day of the year and he was gone, the year was over, and he was over; but he was turning at the plane to wave; then she was crying heavily, but still she heard or felt Posy behind her, and she spun around. Posy was holding two logs across her chest, and her face and ears were red from the cold. Then her lips began to quiver and she dropped the logs. Ellen went to her knees and pressed Posy to her breast, crying: 'Oh, Pete! She knew too! She knew too!'

And she hugged Posy even more tightly, as if for all time.

PART THREE

Adultery

... love is a direction and not a state of the soul.
Simone Weil, *Waiting on God*

to Gina Berriault

W HEN THEY have finished eating Edith tells Sharon to clear the table then brush her teeth and put on her pajamas; she brings Hank his coffee, then decides she can have a cup too, that it won't keep her awake because there is a long evening ahead, and she pours a cup for herself and returns to the table. When Sharon has gone upstairs Edith says: 'I'm going to see Joe.'

Hank nods, sips his coffee, and looks at his watch. They have been silent during most of the meal but after her saying she is going to see Joe the silence is uncomfortable.

'Do you have to work tonight?' she says.

'I have to grade a few papers and read one story. But I'll read to Sharon first.'

Edith looks with muted longing at his handlebar moustache, his wide neck, and thick wrists. She is lighting a cigarette when Sharon comes downstairs in pajamas.

'Daddy quit,' Sharon says, 'Why don't you quit?'

Edith smiles at her, and shrugs.

'I'm going out for awhile,' she says. 'To see a friend.'

Sharon's face straightens with quick disappointment that borders on an angry sense of betrayal.

'What friend?'

'Terry,' Edith says.

'Why can't she come here?'

'Because Daddy has work to do and we want to talk.'

'I'll read to you,' Hank says.

Sharon's face brightens.

'What will you read?'

'Kipling.'

'"Rikki-Tikki-Tavi"?'

'Yes: "Rikki-Tikki-Tavi."'

She is eight and Edith wonders how long it will be before Sharon senses and understands that other presence or absence that Edith feels so often when the family is together. She leaves the table, puts the dishes and pots in the dishwasher, and turns it on. She is small and slender and she is conscious of her size as she puts on her heavy coat. She goes to the living room and kisses Hank and Sharon, but she does not leave through the front door. She goes to the kitchen and takes from the refrigerator the shrimp wrapped in white paper; she goes out the back door, into the dark. A light snow has started to fall.

It is seven-thirty. She has told Joe not to eat until she gets there, because she wants to cook shrimp scampi for him. She likes cooking for Joe, and she does it as often as she can. Wreathed in the smells of cooking she feels again what she once felt as a wife: that her certain hands are preparing a gift. But there were times, in Joe's kitchen, when this sense of giving was anchored in vengeful images of Hank, and then she stood in the uncertainty and loss of meaningless steam and smells. But that doesn't happen anymore. Since Joe started to die, she has been certain about everything she does with him. She has not felt that way about anyone, even Sharon, for a long time.

The snow is not heavy but she drives slowly, cautiously, through town. It is a small town on the Merrimack River, and tonight there are few cars on the road. Leaving town she enters the two-lane country road that will take her to Joe. She tightens her seat belt, turns on the radio, lights a cigarette, and knows that none of these measures will slow the tempo of her heart. The road curves through pale meadows and dark trees and she is alone on it. Then there are houses again, distanced from each other by hills and fields, and at the third one, its front porch lighted, she turns into the driveway. She turns on the interior light, looks at her face in the rearview mirror, then goes up the shovelled walk, her face lowered from the snow, and for a moment she sees herself as Joe will see her coming inside with cheeks flushed and droplets in her long black hair. Seeing herself that way, she feels loved. She is thirty years old.

When Joe opens the door she feels the awkward futility of the shrimp in her hand. She knows he will not be able to eat tonight. He has lost thirty pounds since the night last summer when they got drunk and the next day he was sick and the day after and the day after, so that finally he could not blame it on gin and he went to a doctor and then to the hospital where a week later they removed one kidney with its envelope of cancer that had already spread upward. During the X-ray treatments in the fall, five days a week for five weeks, with the square drawn in purple marker on his chest so the technician would know where to aim, he was always nauseated. But when the treatments were finished there were nights when he could drink and eat as he used to. Other nights he could not. Tonight is one of those: above his black turtleneck the pallor of his face is sharpened; looking from that flesh his pale blue eyes seem brighter than she knows they are. His forehead is moist; he is forty years old, and his hair has been grey since his mid-thirties. He holds her, but even as he squeezes her to him, she feels him pulling his body back from the embrace, so she knows there is pain too. Yet still he holds her tightly so his pulling away causes only a stiffening of his torso while his chest presses against her. She remembers the purple square and is glad it is gone now. She kisses him.

'I'm sorry about the shrimp,' he says. 'I don't think I can eat them.'

'It's all right; they'll keep.'

'Maybe tomorrow.'

'Maybe so.'

The apartment is small, half of the first floor of a small two-story house, and it is the place of a man who since his boyhood has not lived with a woman except housekeepers in rectories. The front room where they are standing, holding each other lightly now like dancers, is functional and, in a masculine disorderly way, orderly; it is also dirty. Fluffs of dust have accumulated on the floor. Edith decides to bring over her vacuum cleaner tomorrow. She puts her coat on a chair and moves through the room and down the short hall toward the kitchen; as she passes his bedroom she glances at the bed to see if he rested before she came; if he did, he has concealed it: the spread is smooth. She wonders how he spent his day, but she is afraid to ask. The college is still paying him, though someone else is teaching his philosophy courses that he started in the fall and had to quit after three days. She puts the shrimp in the refrigerator; always, since they were first lovers, when she looks in his refrigerator she feels a tenderness whose edges touch both amusement and pathos. The refrigerator is clean, it has four ice trays, and it holds only the makings of breakfast and cocktail hour. Behind her he is talking: this afternoon he took a short walk in the woods; he sat on a log and watched a cock pheasant walking across a clearing, its feathers fluffed against the cold. The land is posted and pheasants live there all winter. After the walk he tried to read Unamuno but finally he listened to Rachmaninoff and watched the sun setting behind the trees.

While he gets ice and pours bourbon she looks around the kitchen for signs. In the dish drainer are a bowl, a glass, and a spoon and she hopes they are from lunch, soup and milk, but she thinks they are from breakfast. He gives her the drink and opens a can of beer for himself. When he feels well he drinks gin; once he told her he'd always loved gin and that's why he'd never been a whiskey priest.

'Have you eaten since breakfast?'

'No,' he says, and his eyes look like those of a liar. Yet he and Edith never lie to each other. It is simply that they avoid the words cancer and death and time, and when they speak of his symptoms they are looking at the real words like a ghost between them. At the beginning she saw it only in his eyes: while he joked and smiled his eyes saw the ghost and she did too, and she felt isolated by her health and hope. But gradually, as she forced herself to look at his eyes, the ghost became hers too. It filled his apartment: she looked through it at the food she cooked and they ate; she looked through it at the drinks she took from his hand; it was between them when they made love in the dark of the bedroom and afterward when she lay beside him and her eyes adjusted to the dark and discerned the outlines and shapes of the chest of drawers against the wall at the foot of the bed and, hanging above it, the long black crucifix, long enough to hang in the classroom of a parochial school, making her believe Joe had taken with him from the priesthood a crucifix whose size would assert itself on his nights. When they went to restaurants and bars she looked through the ghost at other couples; it delineated these people, froze their gestures in time. One night, looking in his bathroom mirror, she saw that it was in her own eyes. She wondered what Joe's eyes saw when they were closed, in sleep.

'You should eat,' she says.

'Yes.'

'Do you have something light I could fix?'

'My body.' He pats his waist; he used to have a paunch; when he lost the weight he bought clothes and now all his slacks are new.

'Your head will be light if you take walks and don't eat and then drink beer.'

He drinks and smiles at her.

'Nag.'

'Nagaina. She's the mother cobra. In 'Rikki-Tikki-Tavi.' Would you eat some soup?'

'I would. I was wondering first—' (His eyes start to lower but he raises them again, looks at her) '—if you'd play trainer for a while. Then maybe I'd take some soup.'

'Sure. Go lie down.'

She gets the heating ointment from the medicine cabinet in the bathroom; it lies beside the bottle of sleeping pills. On the shelf beneath these are his shaving cream, razor, after-shave lotion, and stick deodorant. The juxtaposition disturbs her, and for a moment she succumbs to the heavy weariness of depression. She looks at her hand holding the tube of ointment. The hand does not seem to be hers; or, if it is, it has no function, it is near atrophy, it can touch no one. She lowers the hand out of her vision, closes the cabinet door, and looks at herself in the mirror. She is pretty. The past three years show in her face, but still she is pretty and she sips her drink and thinks of Joe waiting and her fingers caress the tube.

In the bedroom Joe is lying on his back, with his shirt off. The bedside lamp is on. He rolls on his belly and turns his face on the pillow so he can watch her. She lights him a cigarette then swallows the last of her bourbon and feels it. Looking at his back she unscrews the cap from the tube; his flesh is pale and she wishes it were summer so she could take him to the beach and lie beside him and watch his skin assume a semblance of health. She squeezes ointment onto her fingers and gently rubs it into the flesh where his kidney used to be. She is overtaken by a romantic impulse which means nothing in the face of what they are facing: she wishes there were no cancer but that his other kidney was in danger and he needed hers and if only he had hers he would live. Her hands move higher on his back. He lies there and smokes, and they do not talk. The first time she rubbed his back they were silent because he had not wanted to ask her to but he had anyway; and she had not wanted to do it but she had, and her flesh had winced as she touched him, and he had known it and she had known that he did. After that, on nights when she sensed his pain, or when he told her about it, she rose from the bed and got the ointment and they were silent, absorbing the achieved intimacy of her flesh. Now his eyes are closed and she watches his face on the pillow and feels what she is heating with her anointed hands.

When she is done she warms a can of vegetable soup and toasts a slice of bread. As she stirs the soup she feels him watching from the table behind her. He belches and blames it on the beer and she turns to him and smiles. She brings him the bowl of soup, the toast, and a glass of milk. She puts ice in her glass and pours bourbon, pouring with a quick and angry turning of the wrist that is either defiant or despairing—she doesn't know which. She sits with him. She would like to smoke but she knows it bothers him while he is eating so she waits. But he does not finish the soup. He eats some of the toast and drinks some of the milk and pretends to wait for the soup to cool; under her eyes he eats most of the soup and finishes the toast and is lifting a spoonful to his mouth when his face is suffused with weariness and resignation which change as quickly to anger as he shakes his head and lowers the spoon, his eyes for a moment glaring at her (but she knows it isn't her he sees) before he pushes back from the table and moves fast out of the kitchen and down the hall. She follows and is with him when he reaches the toilet and standing behind him she holds his waist with one arm and his forehead with her hand. They are there for a long time and she doesn't ask but knows he was here after breakfast and perhaps later in the day. She thinks of him alone retching and quivering over the toilet. Still holding his waist she takes a washcloth from the towel rack and reaches to the lavatory and dampens it; she presses it against his forehead. When he is finished she walks with him to the bedroom, her arm around his waist, his around her shoulder, and she pulls back the covers while he undresses. The telephone is on the bedside table. He gets into bed and she covers him then turning her back to him she dials her home. When Hank answers she says: 'I might stay a while.'

'How is he?'

She doesn't answer. She clamps her teeth and shuts her eyes and raising her left hand she pushes her hair back from her face and quickly wipes the tears from beneath her eyes.

'Bad?' Hank says.

'Yes.'

'Stay as long as you want,' he says. His voice is tender and for a moment she responds to that; but she has been married to him for eight years and known him for the past three and the moment passes; she squeezes the phone and wants to hit him with it.

She goes to the kitchen, the bathroom, and the living room, getting her drink and turning out lights. Joe is lying on his belly with his eyes closed. She undresses, hoping he will open his eyes and see her; she is the only woman he has ever made love with and always he has liked watching her undress; but he does not open his eyes. She turns out the lamp and goes around the bed and gets in with her drink. Propped on a pillow she finishes it and lowers the glass to the floor as he holds her hand. He remains quiet and she can feel him talking to her in his mind. She moves closer to him, smelling mouthwash and ointment, and she thinks of the first time they made love and the next day he bought a second pillow and two satin pillowcases and that night showing them to her he laughed and said he felt like Gatsby with his shirts. She said: Don't make me into that Buchanan bitch; I don't leave bodies in the road. Months later when she went to the hospital to see him after the operation she remembered what she had said. Still, and strangely, there is a sad but definite pleasure remembering him buying the pillow and two satin pillowcases.

Suddenly he is asleep. It happens so quickly that she is afraid. She listens to his slow breath and then, outstretched beside him, touching as much of the length of his body as she can, she closes her eyes and prays to the dark above her. She feels that her prayers do not ascend, that they disseminate in the dark beneath the ceiling. She does not use words, for she cannot feel God above the bed. She prays with images: she sees Joe suffering in a hospital bed with tubes in his body and she does not want him to suffer. So finally her prayer is an image of her sitting beside this bed holding his hand while, gazing at her peacefully and without pain, he dies. But this doesn't touch the great well of her need and she wishes she could know the words for all of her need and that her statement would rise through and beyond the ceiling, up beyond the snow and stars, until it reached an ear. Then listening to Joe's breathing she begins to relax, and soon she sleeps. Some time in the night she is waked by his hands. He doesn't speak. His breath is quick and he kisses her and enters with a thrust she receives; she feels him arcing like Icarus, and when he collapses on her and presses his lips to her throat she knows she holds his entire history in her body. It has been a long time since she has felt this with a man. Perhaps she never has.

§2

ALL SHE HAD ever wanted to be was a nice girl someone would want to marry. When she married Hank Allison she was twenty-two years old and she had not thought of other possibilities. Husbands died, but one didn't think of that. Marriages died too: she had seen enough corpses and heard enough autopsies in Winnetka (the women speaking: sipping their drinks, some of them afraid, some fascinated as though by lust; no other conversation involved them so; Edith could feel flesh in the room, pores, blood, as they spoke of what had destroyed or set free one of their kind); so she knew about the death of love as she knew about breast cancer. And, just as she touched and explored her breasts, she fondled her marriage, stroked that space of light and air that separated her from Hank.

He was her first lover; they married a year earlier than they had planned because she was pregnant. From the time she missed her first period until she went to the gynecologist she was afraid and Hank was too; every night he came to her apartment and the first thing he asked was whether she had started. Then he drank and talked about his work and the worry left his eyes. After she had gone to the doctor she was afraid for another week or so; Hank's eyes pushed her further into herself. But after a while he was able to joke about it. We should have done it right, he said—gone to the senior prom and made it in the car. He was merry and resilient. In her bed he grinned and said the gods had caught up with him for all the times he'd screwed like a stray dog.

When she was certain Hank did not feel trapped she no longer felt trapped, and she became happy about having a child. She phoned her parents. They seemed neither alarmed nor unhappy. They liked Hank and, though Edith had never told them, she knew they had guessed she and Hank were lovers. She drove up to Winnetka to plan the wedding. While her father was at work or gone to bed she had prenatal conversations with her mother. They spoke of breast-feeding, diet, smoking, natural childbirth, saddleblocks. Edith didn't recognize the significance of these conversations until much later, in her ninth month. They meant that her marriage had begun at the moment when she was first happy about carrying a child. She was no longer Hank's lover; she was his wife. What had been clandestine and sweet and dark was now open; the fruit of that intimacy was shared with her mother. She had begun to nest. Before the wedding she drove back to Iowa City, where Hank was a graduate student, and found and rented a small house. There was a room where Hank could write and there was a room for the baby, as it grew older. There was a back yard with an elm tree. She had money from her parents, and spent a few days buying things to put in the house. People delivered them. It was simple and comforting.

In her ninth month, looking back on that time, she began to worry about Hank. Her life had changed, had entered a trajectory of pregnancy and motherhood; his life had merely shifted to the side, to make more room. But she began to wonder if he had merely shifted. Where was he, who was he, while she talked with her mother, bought a washing machine, and felt the baby growing inside her? At first she worried that he had been left out, or anyway felt left out; that his shifting aside had involved enormous steps. Then at last she worried that he had not shifted at all but, for his own survival, had turned away.

She became frightened. She remembered how they had planned marriage: it would come when he finished school, got a job. They used to talk about it. Hank lived in one room of an old brick building which was owned by a cantankerous and colorful old man who walked with the assistance of a stout, gnarled, and threatening cane; like most colorful people, he knew he was and he used that quality, in his dealings with student-tenants, to balance his cantankerousness, which he was also aware of and could have controlled but instead indulged, the way some people indulge their vicious and beloved dogs. In the old brick house there was one communal kitchen, downstairs; it was always dirty and the refrigerator was usually empty because people tended to eat whatever they found there, even if the owner had attached a note to it asking that it be spared.

Edith did not cook for Hank in that kitchen. When she cooked for him, and she liked to do that often, she did it in her own apartment, in a tiny stifling kitchen that was little more than an alcove never meant to hold the refrigerator and stove, which faced each other and could not be opened at the same time. Her apartment itself was narrow, a room on one side of a house belonging to a tense young lawyer and his tenser young wife and their two loud sons who seemed oblivious to that quality which permeated their parents' lives. Neither the lawyer nor his wife had ever told Edith she could not keep a man overnight. But she knew she could not. She knew this because they did not drink or smoke or laugh very much either, and because of the perturbed lust in the lawyer's eyes when he glanced at her. So she and Hank made love on the couch that unfolded and became a narrow bed, and then he went home. He didn't want to spend the night anyway, except on some nights when he was drunk. Since he was a young writer in a graduate school whose only demand was that he write, and write well, he was often drunk, either because he had written well that day or had not. But he was rarely so drunk that he wanted to stay the night at Edith's. And, when he did, it wasn't because liquor had released in him some need he wouldn't ordinarily yield to; it was because he didn't want to drive home. Always, though, she got him out of the house; and always he was glad next morning that she had.

He had little money, only what an assistantship gave him, and he didn't like her to pay for their evenings out, so when they saw each other at night it was most often at her apartment. Usually before he came she would shower and put on a dress or skirt. He teased her about that but she knew he liked it. So did she. She liked being dressed and smelling of perfume and brushing her long black hair before the mirror, and she liked the look in his eyes and the way his voice heightened and belied his teasing. She put on records and they had drinks and told each other what they had done that day. She was pretending to be in her first year of graduate school, in American history, so she could be near Hank; she attended classes, even read the books and wrote the papers, even did rather well; but she was pretending. They drank for a while, then she stood between the hot stove and the refrigerator and cooked while he stood at the entrance of the alcove, and they talked. They ate at a small table against the wall of the living room; the only other room was the bathroom. After dinner she washed the dishes, put away leftovers in foil, and they unfolded the couch and made love and lay talking until they were ready to make love again. It all felt like marriage. Even at twenty-seven, looking back on those nights after five years of marriage, she still saw in them what marriage could often be: talk and dinner and, the child asleep, living-room lovemaking long before the eleven o'clock news which had become their electronic foreplay, the weather report the final signal to climb the stairs together and undress.

On those nights in the apartment they spoke of marriage. And he explained why, even on the nights of Iowa winter when his moustache froze as he walked from her door around the lawyer's house and down the slippery driveway to his car, he did not want to spend the night with her. It was a matter of ritual, he told her. It had to do with his work. He did not want to wake up with someone (he said *someone*, not *you*) and then drive home to his own room where he would start the morning's work. What he liked to do, he said (already she could see he sometimes confused like to with have to) was spend his first wakeful time of the day alone. In his room, each working morning, he first made his bed and cleared his desk of mail and books, then while he made his coffee and cooked bacon and eggs on the hot plate he read the morning paper; he read through the meal and afterward while he drank coffee and smoked. By the time he had finished the paper and washed the dishes in the bathroom he had been awake for an hour and a half. Then, with the reluctance which began as he reached the final pages of the newspaper, he sat at his desk and started to work.

He spoke so seriously, almost reverently, about making a bed, eating some eggs, and reading a newspaper, that at first Edith was amused; but she stifled it and asked him what was happening during that hour and a half of quiet morning. He said, That's it: quiet: silence. While his body woke he absorbed silence. His work was elusive and difficult and had to be stalked; a phone call or an early visitor could flush it. She said, What about after we're married? He smiled and his arm tightened her against him. He told her of a roommate he had, when he was an undergraduate. The roommate was talkative. He woke up talking and went to bed talking. Most of the talk was good, a lot of it purposely funny, and Hank enjoyed it. Except at breakfast. The roommate liked to share the newspaper with Hank and talk about what they were reading. Hank was writing a novel then; he finished it in his senior year, read it at home that summer in Phoenix, and, with little ceremony or despair, burned it. But he was writing it then, living with the roommate, and after a few weeks of spending an hour and a half cooking, reading, and talking and then another hour in silence at his desk before he could put the first word on paper, he started waking at six o'clock so that his roommate woke at eight to an apartment that smelled of bacon and, walking past Hank's closed door, he entered the kitchen where Hank's plate and fork were in the drainer, the clean skillet on the stove, coffee in the pot, and the newspaper waiting on the table.

So in her ninth month she began worrying about Hank. What had first drawn her to him was his body: in high school he had played football; he was both too light and too serious to play in college; he was short, compact, and hard, and she liked his poised, graceful walk; with yielding hands she liked touching his shoulders and arms. When he told her he ran five miles every day she was pleased. Later, not long before they were lovers, she realized that what she loved about him was his vibrance, intensity; it was not that he was a writer; she had read little and indiscriminately and he would have to teach her those things about his work that she must know. She loved him because he had found his center, and it was that center she began worrying about in her ninth month. For how could a man who didn't want to spend a night with his lover be expected to move into a house with a woman, and then a baby? She watched him.

When he finished the novel, Sharon was two and they were buying a house in Bradford, Massachusetts, where he taught and where Edith believed she could live forever. Boston was forty minutes to the south, and she liked it better than Chicago; the New Hampshire beaches were twenty minutes away; she had been landlocked for twenty-four years and nearly every summer day she took Sharon to the beach while Hank wrote; on sunny days when she let herself get trapped into errands or other trifles that posed as commitments, she felt she had wronged herself; but there were not many of those days. She loved autumn—she and Hank and Sharon drove into New Hampshire and Vermont to look at gold and red and yellow leaves—and she loved winter too—it wasn't as cold and windy as the midwest—and she loved the evergreens and snow on the hills; and all winter she longed for the sea, and some days she bundled up Sharon and drove to it and looked at it from the warmth of the car. Then they got out and walked on the beach until Sharon was cold.

Hank was happy about his novel; he sent it to an agent who was happy about it too; but no one else was and, fourteen months later, with more ceremony this time (a page at a time, in the fireplace, three hundred and forty-eight of them) and much more despair, he burned it. That night he drank a lot but was still sober; or sad enough so that all the bourbon did was make him sadder; in bed he held her but he was not really holding her; he lay on his side, his arms around her; but it was she who was holding him. She wanted to make love with him, wanted that to help him, but she knew it would not and he could not. Since sending his novel to the agent he had written three stories; they existed in the mail and on the desks of editors of literary magazines and then in the mail again. And he had been thinking of a novel. He was twenty-six years old. He had been writing for eight years. And that night, lying against her, he told her the eight years were gone forever and had come to nothing. His wide hard body was rigid in her arms; she thought if he could not make love he ought to cry, break that tautness in his body, his soul. But she knew he could not. All those years meant to him, he said, was the thousands of pages, surely over three, maybe over four, he had written: all those drafts, each one draining him only to be stacked in a box or filing cabinet as another draft took its place: all those pages to get the two final drafts of the two novels that had gone into ashes, into the air. He lived now in a total of fifty-eight typed pages, the three stories that lived in trains and on the desks of men he didn't know.

'Start tomorrow,' she said. 'On the new novel.'

For a few moments he was quiet. Then he said: 'I can't. It's three in the morning. I've been drinking for eight hours.'

'Just a page. Or else tomorrow will be terrible. And the day after tomorrow will be worse. You can sleep late, sleep off the booze. I'll take Sharon to the beach, and when I come home you tell me you've written and run with Jack and you feel strong again.'

At the beach next day she knew he was writing and she felt good about that; she knew that last night he had known it was what he had to do; she also knew he needed her to tell him to do it. But she felt defeated too. Last night, although she had fought it, her knowledge of defeat had begun as she held him and felt that tautness which would yield to neither passion nor grief, and she had known it was his insular will that would get him going again, and would deny her a child.

When he finished the novel fourteen months ago she had started waiting for that time—she knew it would be a moment, an hour, a day, no more: perhaps only a moment of his happy assent—when she could conceive. For by this time, though he had never said it, she knew he didn't want another child. And she knew it was not because of anything as practical and as easily solved as money. It was because of the very force in him which had first attracted her, so that after two years of marriage she could think wryly: one thing has to be said about men who've found their center: they're sometimes selfish bastards. She knew he didn't want another child because he believed a baby would interfere with his work. And his believing it would probably make it true.

She knew he was being shortsighted, foolish, and selfish; she knew that, except for the day of birth itself and perhaps a day after, until her mother arrived to care for Sharon, a baby would not prevent, damage, or even interrupt one sentence of all those pages he had to write and she was happy that he wrote and glad to listen to on those nights when he had to read them too; those pages she also resented at times, when after burning three hundred and forty-eight of them he lay in despair and the beginnings of resilience against her body she had given him more than three hundred and forty-eight times, maybe given him a thousand times, and told her all the eight years meant to him were those pages. And she resented them when she knew they would keep her from having a second child; she wanted a son; and it would do no good, she knew, to assure him that he would not lose sleep, that she would get up with the baby in the night.

Because that really wasn't why he didn't want a baby; he probably thought it was; but it wasn't. So if she told him how simple it would be, he still wouldn't want to do it. Because, whether he knew it or not, he was keeping himself in reserve. He had the life he wanted: his teaching schedule gave him free mornings; he had to prepare for classes but he taught novels he knew well and could skim; he had summers off, he had a friend, Jack Linhart, to talk, drink, and run with; he had a woman and a child he loved, and all he wanted now was to write better than he'd ever written before, and it was that he saved himself for. They had never talked about any of this, but she knew it all. She almost felt the same way about her life; but she wanted a son. So she had waited for him to sell his novel, knowing that would be for him a time of exuberance and power, a time out of the fearful drudgery and isolation of his work, and in that spirit he would give her a child. Now she had to wait again.

In the winter and into the spring when snow melted first around the trunks of trees, and the ice on the Merrimack broke into chunks that floated seaward, and the river climbed and rushed, there was a girl. She came uninvited in Christmas season to a party that Edith spent a day preparing; her escort was uninvited too, a law student, a boring one, who came with a married couple who were invited. Later Edith would think of him: if he had to crash the party he should at least have been man enough to keep the girl he crashed with. Her name was Jeanne, she was from France, she was visiting friends in Boston. That was all she was doing: visiting. Edith did not know what part of France she was from nor what she did when she was there. Probably Jeanne told her that night while they stood for perhaps a quarter of an hour in the middle of the room and voices, sipping their drinks, nodding at each other, talking the way two very attractive women will talk at a party: Edith speaking and even answering while her real focus was on Jeanne's short black hair, her sensuous, indolent lips, her brown and mischievous eyes. Edith had talked with the law student long enough—less than a quarter of an hour—to know he wasn't Jeanne's lover and couldn't be; his confidence was still young, wistful, and vulnerable; and there was an impatience, a demand, about the amatory currents she felt flowing from Jeanne. She remarked all of this and recalled nothing they talked about. They parted like two friendly but competing hunters after meeting in the woods. For the rest of the night—while talking, while dancing—Edith watched the law student and the husbands lining up at the trough of Jeanne's accent, and she watched Jeanne's eyes, which appeared vacant until you looked closely at them and saw that they were selfish: Jeanne was watching herself.

And Edith watched Hank, and listened to him. Early in their marriage she had learned to do that. His intimacy with her was private; at their table and in their bed they talked; his intimacy with men was public, and when he was with them he spoke mostly to them, looked mostly at them, and she knew there were times when he was unaware that she or any other woman was in the room. She had long ago stopped resenting this; she had watched the other wives sitting together and talking to one another; she had watched them sit listening while couples were at a dinner table and the women couldn't group so they ate and listened to the men. Usually men who talked to women were trying to make love with them, and she could sense the other men's resentment at this distraction, as if during a hand of poker a man had left the table to phone his mistress. Of course she was able to talk at parties; she wasn't shy and no man had ever intentionally made her feel he was not interested in what she had to say; but willy-nilly they patronized her. As they listened to her she could sense their courtesy, their impatience for her to finish so they could speak again to their comrades. If she had simply given in to that patronizing, stopped talking because she was a woman, she might have become bitter. But she went further: she watched the men, and saw that it wasn't a matter of their not being interested in women. They weren't interested in each other either. At least not in what they said, their ideas; the ideas and witticisms were instead the equipment of friendly, even loving, competition, as for men with different interests were the bowling ball, the putter, the tennis racket. But it went deeper than that too: she finally saw that. Hank needed and loved men, and when he loved them it was because of what they thought and how they lived. He did not measure women that way; he measured them by their sexuality and good sense. He and his friends talked with one another because it was the only way they could show their love; they might reach out and take a woman's hand and stroke it while they leaned forward, talking to men; and their conversations were fields of mutual praise. It no longer bothered her. She knew that some women writhed under these conversations; they were usually women whose husbands rarely spoke to them with the intensity and attention they gave to men.

But that night, listening to Hank, she was frightened and angry. He and Jeanne were watching each other. He talked to the men but he was really talking to her; at first Edith thought he was showing off; but it was worse, more fearful: he was being received and he knew it and that is what gave his voice its exuberant lilt. His eyes met Jeanne's over a shoulder, over the rim of a lifted glass. When Jeanne left with the law student and the invited couple, Edith and Hank told them goodbye at the door. It was only the second time that night Edith and Jeanne had looked at each other and spoken; they smiled and voiced amenities; a drunken husband lurched into the group; his arm groped for Jeanne's waist and his head plunged downward to kiss her. She quickly cocked her head away, caught the kiss lightly on her cheek, almost dodged it completely. For an instant her eyes were impatient. Then that was gone. Tilted away from the husband's muttering face she was looking at Hank. In her eyes Edith saw his passion. She reached out and put an arm about his waist; without looking at him or Jeanne she said goodnight to the law student and the couple. As the four of them went down the walk, shrugging against the cold, she could not look at Jeanne's back and hair; she watched the law student and wished him the disaster of bad grades. Be a bank teller, you bastard.

She did not see Jeanne again. In the flesh, that is. For now she saw her in dreams: not those of sleep which she could forget but her waking dreams. In the mornings Hank went to his office at school to write; at noon he and Jack ran and then ate lunch; he taught all afternoon and then went to the health club for a sauna with Jack and afterward they stopped for a drink; at seven he came home. On Tuesdays and Thursdays he didn't have classes but he spent the afternoon at school in conferences with students; on Saturday mornings he wrote in his office and, because he was free of students that day, he often worked into the middle of the afternoon then called Jack to say he was ready for the run, the sauna, the drinks. For the first time in her marriage Edith thought about how long and how often he was away from home. As she helped Sharon with her boots she saw Jeanne's brown eyes; they were attacking her; they were laughing at her; they sledded down the hill with her and Sharon.

When she became certain that Hank was Jeanne's lover she could not trust her certainty. In the enclosed days of winter she imagined too much. Like a spy, she looked for only one thing, and she could not tell if the wariness in his eyes and voice were truly there; making love with him she felt a distance in his touch, another concern in his heart; passionately she threw herself against that distance and wondered all the time if it existed only in her own quiet and fearful heart. Several times, after drinks at a party, she nearly asked Jack if Hank was always at school when he said he was. At home on Tuesday and Thursday and Saturday afternoons she wanted to call him. One Thursday she did. He didn't answer his office phone; it was a small school and the switchboard operator said if she saw him she'd tell him to call home. Edith was telling Sharon to get her coat, they would go to school to see Daddy, when he phoned. She asked him if he wanted to see a movie that night. He said they had seen everything playing in town and if she wanted to go to Boston he'd rather wait until the weekend. She said that was fine.

In April he and Jack talked about baseball and watched it on television and he started smoking Parliaments. She asked him why. They were milder, he said. He looked directly at her but she sensed he was forcing himself to, testing himself. For months she had imagined his infidelity and fought her imagination with the absence of evidence. Now she had that: she knew it was irrational but it was just rational enough to release the demons: they absorbed her: they gave her certainty. She remembered Jeanne holding a Parliament, waiting for one of the husbands to light it. She lasted three days. On a Thursday afternoon she called the school every hour, feeling the vulnerability of this final prideless crumbling, making her voice as casual as possible to the switchboard operator, even saying once it was nothing important, just something she wanted him to pick up on the way home, and when he got home at seven carrying a damp towel and smelling faintly of gin she knew he had got back in time for the sauna with Jack and had spent the afternoon in Jeanne's bed. She waited until after dinner, when Sharon was in bed. He sat at the kitchen table, talking to her while she cleaned the kitchen. It was a ritual of theirs. She asked him for a drink. Usually she didn't drink after dinner, and he was surprised. Then he said he'd join her. He gave her the bourbon then sat at the table again.

'Are you having an affair with that phony French bitch?'

He sipped his drink, looked at her, and said: 'Yes.'

The talk lasted for days. That night it ended at three in the morning after, straddling him, she made love with him and fell into a sleep whose every moment, next morning, she believed she remembered. She had slept four hours. When she woke to the news on the radio she felt she had not slept at all, that her mind had continued the talk with sleeping Hank. She did not want to get up. In bed she smoked while Hank showered and shaved. At breakfast he did not read the paper. He spoke to Sharon and watched Edith. She did not eat. When he was ready to leave, he leaned down and kissed her and said he loved her and they would talk again that night.

All day she knew what madness was, or she believed she was at least tasting it and at times she yearned for the entire feast. While she did her work and made lunch for Sharon and talked to her and put her to bed with a coloring book and tried to read the newspaper and then a magazine, she could not stop the voices in her mind: some of it repeated from last night, some drawn up from what she believed she had heard and spoken in her sleep, some in anticipation of tonight, living tonight before it was there, so that at two in the afternoon she was already at midnight and time was nothing but how much pain she could feel at once. When Sharon had been in bed for an hour without sleeping Edith took her for a walk and tried to listen to her and said yes and no and I don't know, what do you think? and even heard most of what Sharon said and all the time the voices would not stop. All last night while awake and sleeping and all day she had believed it was because Jeanne was pretty and Hank was a man. Like any cliché, it was easy to live with until she tried to; now she began to realize how little she knew about Hank and how much she suspected and feared, and that night after dinner which she mostly drank she tucked in Sharon and came down to the kitchen and began asking questions. He told her he would stop seeing Jeanne and there was nothing more to talk about; he spoke of privacy. But she had to know everything he felt; she persisted, she harried, and finally he told her she'd better be as tough as her questions were, because she was going to get the answers.

Which were: he did not believe in monogamy. Fidelity, she said. You see? he said. You distort it. He was a faithful husband. He had been discreet, kept his affair secret, had not risked her losing face. He loved her and had taken nothing from her. She accused him of having a double standard and he said no; no, she was as free as she was before she met him. She asked him how long he had felt this way, had he always been like this or was it just some French bullshit he had picked up this winter. He had always felt this way. By now she could not weep. Nor rage either. All she could feel and say was: Why didn't I ever know any of this? You never asked, he said.

It was, she thought, like something bitter from Mother Goose: the woman made the child, the child made the roof, the roof made the

woman, and the child went away. Always she had done her house-
work quickly and easily; by ten-thirty on most mornings she had
done what had to be done. She was not one of those women whose
domesticity became an obsession; it was work that she neither liked
nor disliked and, when other women complained, she was puzzled
and amused and secretly believed their frustration had little to do
with scraping plates or pushing a vacuum cleaner over a rug. Now
in April and May an act of will got her out of bed in the morning.
The air in the house was against her: it seemed wet and grey and
heavy, heavier than fog, and she pushed through it to the bathroom
where she sat staring at the floor or shower curtain long after she
was done; then she moved to the kitchen and as she prepared breakfast the air pushed down on her arms and against her body. *I am
beating eggs*, she said to herself, and she looked down at the fork in
her hand, yolk dripping from the tines into the eggs as their swirl-
ing ceased and they lay still in the bowl. *I am beating eggs*. Then she
jabbed the fork in again. At breakfast Hank read the paper. Edith
talked to Sharon and ate because she had to, because it was morning, it was time to eat, and she glanced at Hank's face over the
newspaper, listened to the crunching of his teeth on toast, and told
herself: *I am talking to Sharon*. She kept her voice sweet, motherly,
attentive.

Then breakfast was over and she was again struck by the seductive waves of paralysis that had washed over her in bed, and she
stayed at the table. Hank kissed her (she turned her lips to him,
they met his, she did not kiss him) and went to the college. She read
the paper and drank coffee and smoked while Sharon played with
toast. She felt she would fall asleep at the table; Hank would return
in the afternoon to find her sleeping there among the plates and
cups and glasses while Sharon played alone in a ditch somewhere
down the road. So once again she rose through an act of will,
watched Sharon brushing her teeth (*I am watching* . . .), sent her to
the cartoons on television, and then slowly, longing for sleep, she
washed the skillet and saucepan (*always scramble eggs in a saucepan*,
her mother had told her; *they stand deeper than in a skillet and they'll
cook softer*) and scraped the plates and put them and the glasses and
cups and silverware in the dishwasher.

Then she carried the vacuum cleaner upstairs and made the bed

Hank had left after she had, and as she leaned over to tuck in the sheet she wanted to give in to the lean, to collapse in slow motion face down on the half-made bed and lie there until—there had been times in her life when she had wanted to sleep until something ended. Unmarried in Iowa, when she missed her period she wanted to sleep until she knew whether she was or not. Now *until* meant nothing. No matter how often or how long she slept she would wake to the same house, the same heavy air that worked against her every move. She made Sharon's bed and started the vacuum cleaner. Always she had done that quickly, not well enough for her mother's eye, but her mother was a Windex housekeeper: a house was not done unless the windows were so clean you couldn't tell whether they were open or closed; but her mother had a cleaning woman. The vacuum cleaner interfered with the cartoons and Sharon came up to tell her and Edith said she wouldn't be long and told Sharon to put on her bathing suit—it was a nice day and they would go to the beach. But the cleaning took her longer than it had before, when she had moved quickly from room to room, without lethargy or boredom but a sense of anticipation, the way she felt when she did other work which required neither skill nor concentration, like chopping onions and grating cheese for a meal she truly wanted to cook.

Now, while Sharon went downstairs again and made lemonade and poured it in the thermos and came upstairs and went down again and came up and said yes there was a little mess and went downstairs and wiped it up, Edith pushed the vacuum cleaner and herself through the rooms and down the hall, and went downstairs and started in the living room while Sharon's voice tugged at her as strongly as hands gripping her clothes, and she clamped her teeth on the sudden shrieks that rose in her throat and told herself: *Don't: she's not the problem;* and she thought of the women in supermarkets and on the street, dragging and herding and all but cursing their children along (one day she had seen a woman kick her small son's rump as she pulled him into a drugstore), and she thought of the women at parties, at dinners, or on blankets at the beach while they watched their children in the waves, saying: *I'm so damned bored with talking to children all day—no,* she told herself, *she's not the problem.* Finally she finished her work, yet she felt none of the relief she had

felt before; the air in the house was like water now as she moved
through it up the stairs to the bedroom, where she undressed and
put on her bathing suit. Taking Sharon's hand and the windbreak-
ers and thermos and blanket, she left the house and blinked in the
late morning sun and wondered near-prayerfully when this would
end, this dread disconnection between herself and what she was
doing. At night making love with Hank she thought of him with
Jeanne, and her heart, which she thought was beyond breaking,
broke again, quickly, easily, as if there weren't much to break any
more, and fell into mute and dreary anger, the dead end of love's
grief.

In the long sunlit evenings and the nights of May the talk was
sometimes philosophical, sometimes dark and painful, drawing
from him details about him and Jeanne; she believed if she pos-
sessed the details she would dispossess Jeanne of Hank's love. But
she knew that wasn't her only reason. Obsessed by her pain, she
had to plunge more deeply into it, feel all of it again and again. But
most of the talk was abstract, and most of it was by Hank. When
she spoke of divorce he calmly told her they had a loving, intimate
marriage. They were, he said, simply experiencing an honest and
healthful breakthrough. She listened to him talk about the un-
natural boundaries of lifelong monogamy. He remained always
calm. Cold, she thought. She could no longer find his heart.
    At times she hated him. Watching him talk she saw his life: with
his work he created his own harmony, and then he used the people
he loved to relax with. Probably it was not exploitative; probably it
was the best he could do. And it was harmony she had lost. Until
now her marriage had been a circle, like its gold symbol on her
finger. Wherever she went she was still inside it. It had a safe,
gentle circumference, and mortality and the other perils lay outside
of it. Often now while Hank slept she lay awake and tried to pray.
She wanted to fall in love with God. She wanted His fingers to
touch her days, to restore meaning to those simple tasks which now
drained her spirit. On those nights when she tried to pray she
longed to leave the world: her actions would appear secular but
they would be her communion with God. Cleaning the house
would be an act of forgiveness and patience under His warm eyes.

But she knew it was no use: she had belief, but not faith: she could not bring God under her roof and into her life. He awaited her death.

Nightly and fearfully now, as though Hank's adulterous heart had opened a breach and let it in to stalk her, she thought of death. One night they went with Jack and Terry Linhart to Boston to hear Judy Collins. The concert hall was filled and darkened and she sat in the sensate, audible silence of listening people and watched Judy under the spotlight in a long lavender gown, her hair falling over one shoulder as she lowered her face over the guitar. Soon Edith could not hear the words of the songs. Sadly she gazed at Judy's face, and listened to the voice, and thought of the voice going out to the ears of all those people, all those strangers, and she thought how ephemeral was a human voice, and how death not only absorbed the words in the air, but absorbed as well the act of making the words, and the time it took to say them. She saw Judy as a small bird singing on a wire, and above her the hawk circled. She remembered reading once of an old man who had been working for twenty-five years sculpting, out of a granite mountain in South Dakota, a 563-foot-high statue of Chief Crazy Horse. She thought of Hank and the novel he was writing now, and as she sat beside him her soul withered away from him and she hoped he would fail, she hoped he would burn this one too: she saw herself helping him, placing alternate pages in the fire. Staring at the face above the lavender gown she strained to receive the words and notes into her body.

She had never lied to Hank and now everything was a lie. Beneath the cooking of a roast, the still affectionate chatting at dinner, the touch of their flesh, was the fact of her afternoons ten miles away in a New Hampshire woods where, on a blanket among shading pines and hemlocks, she lay in sin-quickened heat with Jack Linhart. Her days were delightfully strange, she thought. Hank's betrayal had removed her from the actions that were her life; she had performed them like a weary and disheartened dancer. Now, glancing at Hank reading, she took clothes from the laundry basket at her feet and folded them on the couch, and the folding of a warm towel was a manifestation of her deceit. And, watching him across the room, she felt her separation from him taking shape, filling the space between them like a stone. Within herself she stroked and treasured her lover. She knew she was doing the same to the self she had lost in April.

There was a price to pay. When there had been nothing to lie about in their marriage and she had not lied, she had always felt nestled with Hank; but with everyone else, even her closest friends, she had been aware of that core of her being that no one knew. Now she felt that with Hank. With Jack she recognized yet leaped into their passionate lie: they were rarely together more than twice a week; apart, she longed for him, talked to him in her mind, and vengefully saw him behind her closed eyes as she moved beneath Hank. When she was with Jack their passion burned and distorted their focus. For two hours on the blanket they made love again and again, they made love too much, pushing their bodies to consume the yearning they had borne and to delay the yearning that was waiting. Sometimes under the trees she felt like tired meat. The quiet air which she had broken in the first hour with moans now absorbed only their heavy breath. At those moments she saw with detached clarity that they were both helpless, perhaps even foolish. Jack wanted to escape his marriage; she wanted to live with hers; they drove north to the woods and made love. Then they dressed and drove back to what had brought them there.

This was the first time in her life she had committed herself to sin, and there were times when she felt her secret was venomous. Lying beside Terry at the beach she felt more adulterous than when she lay with Jack, and she believed her sun-lulled conversation was somehow poisoning her friend. When she held Sharon, salty and cold-skinned from the sea, she felt her sin flowing with the warmth of her body into the small wet breast. But more often she was proud. She was able to sin and love at the same time. She was more attentive to Sharon than she had been in April. She did not have to struggle to listen to her, to talk to her. She felt cleansed. And looking at Terry's long red hair as she bent over a child, she felt both close to her yet distant. She did not believe women truly had friends among themselves; school friendships dissolved into marriages; married women thought they had friends until they got divorced and discovered other women were only wives drawn together by their husbands. As much as she and Terry were together, they were not really intimate; they instinctively watched each other. She was certain that Terry would do what she was doing. A few weeks ago she would not have known that. She was proud that she knew it now.

With Hank she loved her lie. She kept it like a fire: some evenings after an afternoon with Jack she elaborately fanned it, looking into Hank's eyes and talking of places she had gone while the sitter stayed with Sharon; at other times she let it burn low, was evasive about how she had spent her day, and when the two couples were together she bantered with Jack, teased him. Once Jack left his pack of Luckies in her car and she brought them home and smoked them. Hank noticed but said nothing. When two cigarettes remained in the pack she put it on the coffee table and left it there. One night she purposely made a mistake: after dinner, while Hank watched a ball game on television, she drank gin while she cleaned the kitchen. She had drunk gin and tonic before dinner and wine with the flounder and now she put tonic in the gin, but not much. From the living room came the announcer's voice, and now and then Hank spoke. She hated his voice; she knew she did not hate him; if she did, she would be able to act, to leave him. She hated his voice tonight because he was talking to ballplayers on the screen and because there was no pain in it while in the kitchen her own voice keened without sound and she worked slowly and finished her drink and mixed another, the gin now doing what she had wanted it to: dissolving all happiness, all peace, all hope for it with Hank and all memory of it with Jack, even the memory of that very afternoon under the trees. Gin-saddened, she felt beyond tears, at the bottom of some abyss where there was no emotion save the quivering knees and fluttering stomach and cold-shrouded heart that told her she was finished. She took the drink into the living room and stood at the door and watched him looking at the screen over his lifted can of beer. He glanced at her, then back at the screen. One hand fingered the pack of Luckies on the table, but he did not take one.

'I wish you hadn't stopped smoking,' she said. 'Sometimes I think you did it so you'd outlive me.'

He looked at her, told her with his eyes that she was drunk, and turned back to the game.

'I've been having an affair with Jack.' He looked at her, his eyes unchanged, perhaps a bit more interested; nothing more. His lips showed nothing, except that she thought they seemed ready to smile. 'We go up to the woods in New Hampshire in the afternoons. Usually twice a week. I like it. I started it. I went after him, at a party. I told him about Jeanne. I kept after him. I knew he was available because he's unhappy with Terry. For a while he was worried about you but I told him you wouldn't mind anyway. He's still your friend, if that worries you. Probably more yours than mine. You don't even look surprised. I suppose you'll tell me you've known it all the time.'

'It wasn't too hard to pick up.'

'So it really wasn't French bullshit. I used to want another child. A son. I wouldn't want to now: have a baby in this.'

'Come here.'

For a few moments, leaning against the doorjamb, she thought of going upstairs and packing her clothes and driving away. The impulse was rooted only in the blur of gin. She knew she would get no farther than the closet where her clothes hung. She walked to the couch and sat beside him. He put his arm around her; for a while she sat rigidly, then she closed her eyes and eased against him and rested her head on his shoulder.

In December after the summer which Hank called the summer of truth, when Edith's affair with Jack Linhart had both started and ended, Hank sold his novel. On a Saturday night they had a celebration party. It was a large party, and some of Hank's students came. His girl friend came with them. Edith had phoned Peter at the radio station Friday and invited him, had assured him it was all right, but he had said he was an old-fashioned guilt-ridden adulterer, and could not handle it. She told him she would see him Sunday afternoon.

The girl friend was nineteen years old and her name was Debbie. She was taller than Edith, she wore suede boots, and she had long blonde hair. She believed she was a secret from everyone but Edith. At the party she drank carefully (only wine), was discreet with Hank, and spent much time talking with Edith, who watched the face that seemed never to have borne pain, and thought: These

Goddamn young girls don't care what they do any more. Hank had said she was a good student. Edith assumed that meant the girl agreed with what he said and told it back to him in different words. What else could come out of a face so untouched? Bland and evil at the same time. Debbie was able to believe it when Hank told her Edith was not jealous. Sometimes Debbie stayed with Sharon while Hank and Edith went out. Hank drove her back to the dormitory; on those nights, by some rule of his own, he did not make love with Debbie. A bit drunk, standing in the kitchen with the girl, Edith glanced at her large breasts stretching the burgundy sweater. How ripe she must be, this young piece. Her nipples thrust against the cashmere. They made love in the car. Hank could not afford motels like Peter could. When Edith was in the car she felt she was in their bed. She looked at the breasts.

'I always wanted big ones,' she murmured.

The girl blushed and took a cigarette from her purse.

'Hank hasn't started smoking again,' Edith said. 'It's amazing.'

'I didn't know he ever did.'

'Until last summer. He wants to live a long time. He wants to publish ten books.'

Edith studied the girl's eyes. They were brown, and showed nothing. A student. Couldn't she understand what she was hearing? That she had come without history into not history, that in a year or more or less she would be gone with her little heart broken or, more than likely, her cold little heart intact, her eyes and lips intact, having given nothing and received less: a memory for Hank to smile over in a moment of a spring afternoon. But then Edith looked away from the eyes. None of this mattered to the girl. Not the parentheses of time, not that blank space between them that one had to fill. It was Edith who would lose. Perhaps the next generation of students would be named Betty or Mary Ann. Well into his forties Hank would be attractive to them. Each year he would pluck what he needed. Salaried and tenured adultery. She would watch them come into her home like ghosts of each other. Sharon would like their attention, as she did now. Edith was twenty-seven. She had ten more years, perhaps thirteen; fifteen. Her looks would be gone. The girls would come with their loose breasts under her roof, and brassiered she would watch them, talk with them. It would not matter to Hank where they had come from and where they were going. He would write books.

She could not read it: the one he sold, the one she had urged him that summer night to begin next day, helping him give birth to it while she gave up a son. When he finished it a month ago and sent it to the agent he gave her the carbon and left her alone with it; it was a Saturday and he went to Jack's to watch football. She tried all afternoon. He needed her to like it; she knew that. He only pretended to care about what she thought of other books or movies. But handing her the manuscript he had boyishly lowered his eyes, and then left. He left because he could not be in the house with her while she read it. When she had read the other one, the one he burned, he had paced about the house and lawn and returned often to watch her face, to see what his work was doing to it. This time he knew better. All of that was in his eyes and voice when he said with such vulnerability that for a moment she wanted to hold him with infinite forgiveness: 'I think I'll go to Jack's and watch the game.'

She tried to recall that vulnerability as she read. But she could not. His prose was objective, concrete, precise. The voice of the book was the voice of the man who last spring and summer had spoken of monogamy, absolved and encouraged her adultery, and in the fall announced that he was having an affair with Debbie. Through the early chapters she was angry. She pushed herself on. Mostly she skimmed. Then she grew sad: this was the way she had wanted it when she first loved him: he would bring her his work and he would need her praise and before anyone else read it the work would be consummated between them. Now she could not read it through the glaze of pain that covered the pages. She skimmed, and when he returned in the evening she greeted him with an awed and tender voice, with brightened eyes; she held him tightly and told him it was a wonderful novel and she thought of how far she had come with this man, how frequent and convincing were her performances.

He wanted to talk about it; he was relieved and joyful; he wanted to hear everything she felt. That was easy enough: they talked for two hours while she cooked and they ate; he would believe afterward that she had talked to him about his book; she had not. Recalling what she skimmed she mentioned a scene or passage, let him interrupt her, and then let him talk about it. Now it would be published, and he would write another. Looking at Debbie she wondered if Peter would leave his wife and marry her. She had not thought of that before; and now, with images in her mind of herself and Peter and Sharon driving away, she knew too clearly what she had known from the beginning: that she did not love Peter Jackman. All adultery is a symptom, she thought. She watched Debbie, who was talking about Hank's novel; she had read it after Edith. Hank brought to his adultery the protocol of a professional. Who *was* this girl? What was she *doing*? Did she put herself to sleep in the dormitory with visions of herself and Hank driving away? In her eyes Edith found nothing; she could have been peering through the windows of a darkened cellar.

'I'm going to circulate,' she said.

In the living room she found Jack, and took his hand. Looking at his eyes she saw their summer and his longing and she touched his cheek and beard and recalled the sun over his shoulder and her hot closed eyes. He did not love Terry but he could not hurt her, nor leave his children, and he was faithful now, he drank too much, and often he talked long and with embittered anger about things of no importance.

'I hope there was *some*thing good,' she said. 'In last summer.'

'There was.' He pressed her hand.

'Doesn't Hank's girl look pretty tonight?' she said.

'I hate the little bitch.'

'So do I.'

Once in Iowa, while Edith was washing clothes at a launderette, a dreary place of graduate students reading, Mann juxtaposed with Tide, and stout wives with curlers in their hair, a place she gladly abandoned when she married Hank and moved into the house with her own washer and dryer, she met a young wife who was from a city in the south. Her husband was a student and he worked nights as a motel clerk. Because they found one for sixty dollars a month, they lived in a farmhouse far from town, far from anyone. From her window at night, across the flat and treeless land, she could see the lights of her closest neighbor, a mile and a half away. She had a small child, a daughter. She had never lived in the country and the farmers liked to tell her frightening stories. While she was getting mail from the box at the road they stopped their tractors and talked to her, these large sunburned farmers who she said had grown to resemble the hogs they raised. They told her of hogs eating drunks and children who fell into the pens. And they told her a year ago during the long bad winter a man had hanged himself in the barn of the house she lived in; he had lived there alone, and he was buried in town.

So at night, while her husband was at the motel desk, the woman was afraid. When she was ready for bed she forced herself to turn off all the downstairs lights, though she wanted to leave every light burning, sleep as if in bright afternoon; then she climbed the stairs and turned out the hall light too, for she was trying to train the child to sleep in the dark. Then she would go to bed and, if she had read long enough, was sleepy enough, she'd go to sleep soon; but always fear was there and if she woke in the night—her bladder, a sound from the child, a lone and rare car on the road in front of the house—she lay terrified in the dark which spoke to her, touched her. In those first wakeful moments she thought she was afraid of the dark itself, that if she dispelled it with light her fear would subside. But she did not turn on the light. And as she lay there she found that within the darkness were spaces of safety. She was not afraid of her room. She lay there a while longer and thought of other rooms. She was not afraid of her child's room. Or the bathroom. Or the hall, the stairs, the living room. It was the kitchen. The shadowed corner between the refrigerator and the cupboard. She did not actually believe someone was crouched there. But it was that corner that she feared. She lay in bed seeing it more clearly than she could see her own darkened room. Then she rose from the bed and, in the dark, went downstairs to the kitchen and stood facing the dark corner, staring at it. She stared at it until she was not afraid; then she went upstairs and slept.

On other nights she was afraid of other places. Sometimes it was the attic, and she climbed the stairs into the stale air, past the dusty window, and stood in the center of the room among boxes and cardboard barrels and knew that a running mouse would send her shouting down the stairs and vowed that it would not. The basement was worse: it was cool and damp, its ceiling was low, and no

matter where she stood there was always a space she couldn't see:
behind the furnace in the middle of the floor, behind the columns
supporting the ceiling. Worst of all was the barn: on some nights
she woke and saw its interior, a dread place even in daylight, with
its beams. She did not know which one he had used; she knew he
had climbed out on one of them, tied the rope, put the noose
around his neck, and jumped. On some nights she had to leave her
bed and go out there. It was autumn then and she only had to put
on her robe and shoes. Crossing the lawn, approaching the wide
dark open door, she was not afraid she would see him: she was
afraid that as she entered the barn she would look up at the beam he
had used and she would know it was the beam he had used.

Driving home Sunday night Edith thought of the woman—she
could not remember her name, only her story—caught as an adult
in the fears of childhood: for it was not the hanged man's ghost she
feared; she did not believe in ghosts. It was the dark. A certain dark
place on a certain night. She had gone to the place and looked at
what she feared. But there was something incomplete about the
story, something Edith had not thought of until now: the woman
had looked at the place where that night her fear took shape. But
she had not discovered what she was afraid of.

In daylight while Hank and Sharon were sledding Edith had
driven to the bar to meet Peter. They had gone to the motel while
the December sun that stayed low and skirting was already down.
When he drove her back to the bar she did not want to leave him
and drive home in the night. She kissed him and held him tightly.
She wanted to go in for a drink but she didn't ask, for she knew he
was late now; he had to return to his wife. His marriage was falling
slowly, like a feather. He thought his wife had a lover (she had had
others), but they kept their affairs secret from each other. Or tried
to. Or pretended to. Edith knew they were merely getting by with
flimsy deception while they avoided the final confrontation. Edith
had never met Norma, or seen her. In the motels Peter talked about
her. She released him and got out of the car and crossed the parking
lot in the dark.

She buckled her seatbelt and turned on the radio and cautiously
joined the traffic on the highway. But it was not a wreck she was
afraid of. The music was bad: repetitious rock from a station for

teenagers. It was the only station she could get and she left it on. She had a thirty-minute drive and she did not know why, for the first time in her adult life, she was afraid of being alone in the dark. She had been afraid from the beginning: the first night she left Peter at a parking lot outside a bar and drove home; and now when Sharon was asleep and Hank was out she was afraid in the house and one night alone she heard the washing machine stop in the basement but she could not go down there and put the clothes in the dryer. Sometimes on grey afternoons she was frightened and she would go to the room where Sharon was and sit with her. Once when Sharon was at a birthday party she fell asleep in late afternoon and woke alone with dusk at the windows and fled through the house turning on lights and Peter's disc-jockey program and fire for the teakettle. Now she was driving on a lovely country road through woods and white hills shimmering under the moon. But she watched only the slick dark road. She thought of the beach and the long blue afternoons and evenings of summer. She thought of grilling three steaks in the back yard. She and Hank and Sharon would be sunburned, their bodies warm and smelling of the sea. They would eat at the picnic table in the seven o'clock sun.

She hoped Hank would be awake when she got home. He would look up from his book, his eyes amused and arrogant as they always were when she returned from her nights. She hoped he was awake. For if he was already asleep she would in silence ascend the stairs and undress in the dark and lie beside him unable to sleep and she would feel the house enclosing and caressing her with some fear she could not name.

§3

BEFORE Joe Ritchie was dying they lay together in the cool nights of spring and he talked. His virginal, long-stored and (he told her) near-atrophied passion leaped and quivered inside her; during the lulls he talked with the effusion of a man who had lived forty years without being intimate with a woman. Which was, he said, pretty much a case of having never been intimate with anyone at all. It was why he left the priesthood. Edith looked beyond the foot of the bed and above the chest of drawers at the silhouette of the hanging crucifix while he told her of what he called his failures, and the yearnings they caused.

He said he had never doubted. When he consecrated he knew that he held the body, the blood. He did not feel proud or particularly humble either; just awed. It was happening in his two lifted hands (and he lifted them above his large and naked chest in the dark), his two hands, of his body; yet at the same time it was not of his body. He knew some priests who doubted. Their eyes were troubled, sometimes furtive. They kept busy: some were athletic, and did that; some read a lot, and others were active in the parish: organized and supervised fairs, started discussion groups, youth groups, pre-Cana groups, married groups, counselled, made sick calls, jail calls, anything to keep them from themselves. Some entered the service, became chaplains. One of them was reported lost at sea. He had been flying with a navy pilot, from a carrier. The poor bastard, Joe said. You know what I think? He wanted to be with that pilot, so he could be around certainty. Watch the man and the machine. A chaplain in an airplane. When I got the word I thought: That's it: in the destructive element immerse, you poor bastard.

Joe had loved the Eucharist since he was a boy; it was why he became a priest. Some went to the seminary to be pastors and bishops; they didn't know it, but it was why they went, and in the seminary they were like young officers. Some, he said, went to pad and shelter their neuroses—or give direction to them. They had a joke then, the young students with their fresh and hopeful faces: behind every Irish priest there's an Irish mother wringing her hands. But most became priests because they wanted to live their lives with God; they had, as the phrase went, a vocation. There were only two vocations, the church taught: the religious life or marriage. Tell that to Hank, she said; he'd sneer at one and laugh at the other. Which would he sneer at? Joe said. I don't really know, she said.

It was a difficult vocation because it demanded a marriage of sorts with a God who showed himself only through the volition, action, imagination, and the resultant faith of the priest himself; when he failed to create and complete his union with God he was thrust back upon himself and his loneliness. For a long time the

Eucharist worked for Joe. It was the high point of his day, when he consecrated and ate and drank. The trouble was it happened early in the morning. He rose and said mass and the day was over, but it was only beginning. That was what he realized or admitted in his mid-thirties: that the morning consecration completed him but it didn't last; there was no other act during the day that gave him that completion, made him feel an action of his performed in time and mortality had transcended both and been received by a God who knew his name.

Of course while performing the tasks of a parish priest he gained the sense of accomplishment which even a conscripted soldier could feel at the end of a chore. Sometimes the reward was simply that the job was over: that he had smiled and chatted through two and a half hours of bingo without displaying his weariness that bordered on panic. But with another duty came a reward that was insidious: he knew that he was a good speaker, that his sermons were better than those of the pastor and the two younger priests. One of the younger priests should have been excused altogether from speaking to gathered people. He lacked intelligence, imagination, and style; with sweaty brow he spoke stiffly of old and superfluous truths he had learned as a student. When he was done, he left the pulpit and with great relief and concentration worked through the ritual, toward the moment when he would raise the host. When he did this, and looked up at the Eucharist in his hands, his face was no longer that of the misfit in the pulpit; his jaw was solemn, his eyes firm. Joe pitied him for his lack of talent, for his anxiety each Sunday, for his awareness of each blank face, each shifting body in the church, and his knowledge that what he said was ineffectual and dull.

Yet he also envied the young priest. In the pulpit Joe loved the sound of his own voice: the graceful flow of his words, his imagery, his timing, and the tenor reaches of his passion; his eyes engaged and swept and recorded for his delight the upturned and attentive faces. At the end of his homily he descended from the pulpit, his head lowered, his face set in the seriousness of a man who has just perceived truth. His pose continued as he faced the congregation for the Credo and the prayers of petition; it continued as he ascended the three steps to the altar and began the offertory and prepared to consecrate. In his struggle to rid himself of the pose, he assumed another: he acted like a priest who was about to hold the body of Christ in his hands, while all the time, even as he raised the host and then the chalice, his heart swelled and beat with love for himself. On the other six days, at the sparsely attended week-day masses without sermons, he broke the silence of the early mornings only with prayers, and unaware of the daily communicants, the same people usually, most of them old women who smelled of sleep and cleanliness and time, he was absorbed by the ritual, the ritual became him, and in the privacy of his soul he ate the body and drank the blood; he ascended; and then his day was over.

The remaining hours were dutiful, and he accepted them with a commitment that nearly always lacked emotion. After a few years he began to yearn; for months, perhaps a year or more, he did not know what he yearned for. Perhaps he was afraid to know. At night he drank more; sometimes the gin curbed his longings that still he wouldn't name; but usually, with drinking, he grew sad. He did not get drunk, so in the morning he woke without hangover or lapse of memory, and recalling last night's gloom he wondered at its source, as though he were trying to understand not himself but a close friend. One night he did drink too much, alone, the pastor and the two younger priests long asleep, Joe going down the hall to the kitchen with less and less caution, the cracking sound of the ice tray in his hands nothing compared to the sound that only he could hear: his monologue with himself; and it was so intense that he felt anyone who passed the kitchen door would hear the voice that resounded in his skull. In the morning he did not recall what he talked about while he drank. He woke dehydrated and remorseful, his mind so dissipated that he had to talk himself through each step of his preparation for the day, for if he didn't focus carefully on buttoning his shirt, tying his shoes, brushing his teeth, he might fall again into the shards of last night. His sleep had been heavy and drunken, his dreams anxious. He was thankful that he could not recall them. He wished he could not recall what he did as he got into bed: lying on his side he had hugged a pillow to his breast, and holding it in both arms had left consciousness saying to himself, to the pillow, to God, and perhaps aloud: I must have a woman.

Leaving the rectory, crossing the lawn to the church in the cool morning, where he would say mass not for the old ladies but for himself, he vowed that he would not get drunk again.

It was not his holding the pillow that frightened him; nor was it the words he had spoken either aloud or within his soul: it was the fearful and ascendant freedom he had felt as he listened to and saw the words. There was dew on the grass beneath his feet; he stopped and looked down at the flecks of it on his polished black shoes. He stood for a moment, a slight cool breeze touching his flesh, the early warmth of the sun on his hair and face, and he felt a loving and plaintive union with all those alive and dead who had at one time in their lives, through drink or rage or passion, suddenly made the statement whose result they had both feared and hoped for and had therefore long suppressed. He imagined a multitude of voices and pained and determined faces, leaping into separation and solitude and fear and hope. His hand rose to his hair, grey in his thirties. He walked on to the church. As he put on his vestments he looked down at the sleepy altar boy, a child. He wanted to touch him but was afraid to. He spoke gently to the boy, touched him with words. They filed into the church, and the old women and a young couple who were engaged and one old man rose.

There were ten of them. With his gin-dried mouth he voiced the prayers while his anticipatory heart beat toward that decision he knew he would one day reach, and had been reaching for some time, as though his soul had taken its own direction while his body and voice moved through the work of the parish. When the ten filed up to receive communion and he placed the host on their tongues and smelled their mouths and bodies and clothes, the sterile old ones and the young couple smelling washed as though for a date, the boy of after-shave lotion, the girl of scented soap, he studied each face for a sign. The couple were too young. In the wrinkled faces of the old he could see only an accumulation of time, of experience; he could not tell whether, beneath those faces, there was a vague recollection of a rewarding life or weary and muted self-contempt because of moments denied, choices run from. He could not tell whether any of them had reached and then denied or followed an admission like the one that gin had drawn from him the night before. Their tongues wet his fingers. He watched them with the dread, excitement, and vulnerability of a man who knows his life is about to change.

After that he stayed sober. The gin had done its work. Before dinner he approached the bottle conspiratorially, held it and looked at it as though it contained a benevolent yet demanding genie. He did not even have to drink carefully. He did not have to drink at all. He drank to achieve a warm nimbus for his secret that soon he would bare to the pastor. In the weeks that followed his drunken night he gathered up some of his past, looked at it as he had not when it was his present, and smiling at himself he saw that he had been in trouble, and the deepest trouble had been his not knowing that he was in trouble. He saw that while he was delivering his sermons he had been proud, yes; perhaps that wasn't even sinful; perhaps it was natural, even good; but the pride was no longer significant. The real trap of his sermons was that while he spoke he had acted out, soberly and with no sense of desperation, the same yearning that had made him cling to the pillow while drunk. For he realized now that beneath his sermons, even possibly at the source of them, was an abiding desire to expose his soul with all his strengths and vanities and weaknesses to another human being. And, further, the other human being was a woman.

Studying himself from his new distance he learned that while he had scanned the congregation he had of course noted the men's faces; but as attentive, as impressed, as they might be, he brushed them aside, and his eyes moved on to the faces of women. He spoke to them. It was never one face. He saw in all those eyes of all those ages the female reception he had to have: grandmothers and widows and matrons and young wives and young girls all formed a composite woman who loved him.

She came to the confessional too, where he sat profiled to the face behind the veiled window, one hand supporting his forehead and shielding his eyes. He sat and listened to the woman's voice. He had the reputation of being an understanding confessor; he had been told this by many of those people who when speaking to a priest were compelled to talk shop; not theirs: his. Go to Father Ritchie, the women told him at parish gatherings; that's what they all say, Father. He sat and listened to the woman's voice. Usually

the sins were not important; and even when they were he began to
sense that the woman and the ritual of confession had nothing to do
with the woman and her sin. Often the sins of men were pragmatic
and calculated and had to do with money; their adulteries were
restive lapses from their responsibilities as husbands and fathers,
and they confessed them that way, some adding the assurance that
they loved their wives, their children. Some men confessed not
working at their jobs as hard as they could, and giving too little time
to their children. Theirs was a world of responsible action; their
sins were what they considered violations of that responsibility.

But the women lived in a mysterious and amoral region which
both amused and attracted Joe. Their sins were instinctual. They
raged at husbands or children; they fornicated or committed adultery; the closest they came to pragmatic sin was birth control, and
few of them confessed that anymore. It was not celibate lust that
made Joe particularly curious about their sexual sins: it was the
vision these sins gave him of their natures. Sometimes he wondered
if they were capable of sinning at all. Husbands whispered of one-
night stands, and in their voices Joe could hear self-reproach that
was rooted in how they saw themselves as part of the world. But
not so with the women. In passion they had made love. There was
no other context for the act. It had nothing to do with their husbands or their children; Joe never said it in the confessional but it
was clear to him that it had nothing to do with God either. He
began to see God and the church and those activities that he
thought of as the world—education, business, politics—as male and
serious, perhaps comically so; while women were their own tem-
ples and walked cryptic, oblivious, and brooding across the earth.
Behind the veil their voices whispered without remorse. Their con-
fessions were a distant and dutiful salute to the rules and patterns of
men. He sat and listened to the woman's voice.

And his reputation was real: he was indeed understanding and
kind, but not for God, not for the sacrament that demanded of him
empathy and compassion as God might have; or Christ. For it was
not God he loved, it was Christ: God in the flesh that each morning
he touched and ate, making his willful and faithful connection with
what he could neither touch nor see. But his awareness of his duty
to imitate Christ was not the source of his virtues as a confessor.

Now, as he prepared to leave the priesthood, he saw that he had given kindness and compassion and understanding because he had wanted to expose that part of himself, real or false, to a faceless nameless woman who would at least know his name because it hung outside the confessional door. And he understood why on that hungover morning he had wanted to touch the altar boy but had been afraid to, though until then his hands had instinctively gone out to children, to touch, to caress; on that morning he had been afraid he would not stop at a touch; that he would embrace the boy, fiercely, like a father.

He did not lose his faith in the Eucharist. After leaving the priesthood he had daily gone to mass and received what he knew was the body and blood of Christ. He knew it, he told Edith, in the simplest and perhaps most profound way: most profound, he said, because he believed that faith had no more to do with intellect than love did; that touching her he knew he loved her and loving her he touched her; and that his flesh knew God through touch as it had to; that there was no other way it could; that bread and wine becoming body and blood was neither miracle nor mystery, but natural, for it happened within the leap of the heart of man toward the heart of God, a leap caused by the awareness of death. Like us, he had said. Like us what? she said, lying beside him last spring, his seed swimming in her, thinking of her Episcopal childhood, she and her family Christian by skin color and pragmatic in belief. When we make love, he said. We do it in the face of death. (And this was in the spring, before he knew.) Our bodies aren't just meat then; they become statement too; they become spirit. If we can do that with each other then why can't we do it with God, and he with us? I don't know, she said; I've never thought about it. Don't, he said; it's too simple.

After they became lovers he continued going to daily mass but he stopped receiving communion. She offered to stop seeing him, to let him confess and return to his sacrament. He told him no. It was not that he believed he was sinning with her; it was that he didn't know. And if indeed he were living in sin it was too complex for him to enter a confessional and simply murmur the word *adultery*; too complex for him to burden just any priest with, in any confessional. He recognized this as pride: the sinner assuming the anonymous confessor would be unable to understand and unwilling to grapple with the extent and perhaps even the exonerating circumstances of the sin, but would instead have to retreat and cling to the word *adultery* and the divine law forbidding it. So he did not confess. And there were times at daily mass when he nearly joined the others and received communion, because he felt that he could, that it would be all right. But he did not trust what he felt: in his love for Edith he was untroubled and happy but he did not trust himself enough to believe he could only be happy within the grace of God. It could be, he told her, that his long and celibate need for earthly love now satisfied, he had chosen to complete himself outside the corridor leading to God; that he was not really a spiritual man but was capable of, if not turning his back on God, at least glancing off to one side and keeping that glance fixed for as long as he and Edith loved. So he did not receive, even though at times he felt that he could.

If she were not married he was certain he would receive communion daily while remaining her lover because, although he knew it was rarely true, he maintained and was committed to the belief that making love could parallel and even merge with the impetus and completion of the Eucharist. Else why make love at all, he said, except for meat in meat, making ourselves meat, drawing our circle of mortality not around each other but around our own vain and separate hearts. But if she were free to love him, each act between them would become a sacrament, each act a sign of their growing union in the face of God and death, freed of their now-imposed limitations on commitment and risk and hope. Because he believed in love, he said. With all his heart he believed in it, saw it as a microcosm of the Eucharist which in turn was a microcosm of the earth-rooted love he must feel for God in order to live with certainty as a man. And like his love for God, his love for her had little to do with the emotion which at times pulsated and quivered in his breast so fiercely that he had to make love with her in order to bear it; but it had more to do with the acts themselves, and love finally was a series of gestures with escalating and enduring commitments.

So if she were free to love him he could receive communion too, take part without contradiction in that gesture too. And if their adultery were the classic variety involving cuckoldry he would know quite simply it was a sin, because for his own needs he would be inflicting pain on a man who loved his wife. But since her marriage was not in his eyes a marriage at all but an arrangement which allowed Hank to indulge his impulses within the shelter of roof, woman, and child which apparently he also needed, the sin—if it existed—was hard to define. So that finally his reason for not receiving communion was his involvement in a marriage he felt was base, perhaps even sordid; and, in love as he was, he reeked or at least smelled faintly of sin, which again he could neither define nor locate; and indeed it could be Hank's sin he carried about with him and shared. Which is why he asked her to marry him.

'It's obvious you love Hank,' he said.

'Yes,' she said, her head on his bare shoulder; then she touched his face, stroked it.

'If you didn't love him you would divorce him, because you could keep Sharon. But your love for him contradicts its purpose. It empties you without filling you, it dissipates you, you'll grow old in pieces.'

'But if I were divorced you couldn't be married in the church. What about your Eucharist? Would you give that up?'

'I'd receive every day,' he said. 'Who would know? I'd go to mass and receive the Eucharist like any other man.'

'I don't think you're a Catholic at all.'

'If I'm not, then I don't know what I am.'

§4

SHE WAKES frightened beside Joe and looks in the grey light at the clock on the bedside table—six-forty. Joe is sleeping on his back, his mouth open; his face seems to have paled and shrunk or sagged during the night, and his shallow breath is liquid. She quietly gets out of bed. Her heart still beats with fright. This is the first time she has ever spent the night with Joe, or with any of her lovers; always the unspoken agreement with Hank was that for the last part of the night and the breakfast hour of the morning the family would be together under one roof; sometimes she had come home as late as four in the morning and gotten into bed beside

Hank, who slept; always when he came home late she was awake and always she pretended she was asleep.

She dresses quickly, watching Joe's face and thinking of Sharon sleeping and hoping she will sleep for another half-hour; although if she wakes and comes down to the kitchen before Edith gets home, Edith can explain that she has been to the store. Yet she knows that discovery by Sharon is not what she really fears, that it will probably be another seven years before Sharon begins to see what she and Hank are doing. At the thought of seven more years of this her fear is instantly replaced by a rush of despair that tightens her jaws in resignation. Then she shakes her head, shakes away the image of those twenty-eight seasons until Sharon is fifteen, and continues to dress; again she is afraid. She needs a cigarette and goes to the kitchen for one; at the kitchen table she writes a note telling Joe she will be back later in the morning. She plans to clean his apartment but does not tell him in the note, which she leaves propped against the bedside clock so he will see it when he wakes and will not have to call her name or get up to see if she is still with him. She writes only that she will be back later and that she loves him. She assumes it is true that she loves him, but for a long time now it has been difficult to sort out her feelings and understand them.

As now, driving home, and knowing it is neither discovery by Sharon nor rebuke by Hank that makes her grip on the wheel so firm and anxious that the muscles of her arms tire from the tension. For she knows Hank will not be disturbed. He likes Joe and will understand why she had to stay the night; although, on the road now, in the pale blue start of the day, her decision to sleep with Joe seems distant and unnecessary, an impulse born in the hyperbole of bourbon and night. She wishes she had gone home after Joe was asleep. But if she is home in time to cook breakfast, Hank will not be angry. So why, then, driving through the streets of a town that she now thinks of as her true home, does she feel like a fugitive? She doesn't know.

And yet the feeling persists through breakfast, even though she is in luck: when she enters the kitchen she hears the shower upstairs; she brings a glass of orange juice upstairs, stopping in her room long enough to hang up her coat and change her sweater and pants;

then she goes to Sharon's room. Sharon sleeps on her back, the long brown hair spread on the pillow, strands of it lying on her upturned cheek; her lips are slightly parted and she seems to be frowning at a dream. The room smells of childhood: the neutral and neuter scents of bedclothes and carpet and wood, and Edith recalls the odors of Joe's apartment, and of Joe. She sits on the side of the bed, pausing to see if her weight will stir Sharon from the dream and sleep. After a while she touches Sharon's cheek; Sharon wakes so quickly, near startled, that Edith is saddened. She likes to watch Sharon wake with the insouciance of a baby, and she regrets her having to get up early and hurry to school. Sharon pushes up on her elbows, half-rising from the bed while her brown eyes are blinking at the morning. Edith kisses her and gives her the juice. Sharon blinks, looks about the room, and asks what time it is.

'There's plenty of time,' Edith says. 'Would you like pancakes?'

Sharon gulps the juice and says yes, then pushes back the covers and is waiting for Edith to get up so she can swing her feet to the floor. Edith kisses her again before leaving the room. In the hall she is drawn to the sound of the shower behind her, needs to say something to Hank, but doesn't know what it is; with both loss and relief she keeps going down the hall and the stairs, into the kitchen.

Hank and Sharon come down together; by this time Edith has made coffee, brought the *Boston Globe* in from the front steps and laid it at Hank's place; the bacon is frying in the iron skillet, the pancake batter is mixed, and the electric skillet is heated. Her eyes meet Hank's. He does not kiss her good-morning before sitting down; that's no longer unusual but this morning the absence of a kiss strikes her like a mild but intended slap. They tell each other good-morning. Since that summer three years ago she has felt with him, after returning from a lover, a variety of emotions which seem unrelated: vengeance, affection, weariness, and sometimes the strange and frightening lust of collusive sin. At times she has also felt shy, and that is how she feels this morning as he props the paper on the milk pitcher, then withdraws it as Sharon lifts the pitcher and pours into her glass. Edith's shyness is no different from what it would be if she and Hank were new lovers, only hours new, and this was the first morning she had waked in his house and as she cooked breakfast her eyes and heart reached out to him to see if this morning he was with her as he was last night. He looks over the paper at her, and his eyes ask about Joe. She shrugs then shakes her head, but she is not thinking of Joe, and the tears that cloud her eyes are not for him either. She pours small discs of batter into the skillet, and turns the bacon. Out of her vision Hank mumbles something to the paper. She breathes the smells of the batter, the bacon, the coffee.

When Hank and Sharon have left, Edith starts her work. There is not much to do, but still she does not take time to read the paper. When she has finished in the kitchen she looks at the guest room, the dining room, and the living room. They are all right; she vacuumed yesterday. She could dust the bookshelves in the living room but she decides they can wait. She goes upstairs; Sharon has made her bed, and Edith smooths it and then makes the other bed where the blankets on her side are still tucked in. The bathroom is clean and smells of Hank's after-shave lotion. He has left hair in the bathtub and whiskers in the lavatory; she picks these up with toilet paper. She would like a shower but she wants to flee from this house. She decides to shower anyway; perhaps the hot water and warm soft lather will calm her. But under the spray she is the same, and she washes quickly and very soon is leaving the house, carrying the vacuum cleaner. On the icy sidewalk she slips and falls hard on her rump. For a moment she sits there, hoping no one has seen her; she feels helpless to do everything she must do; early, the day is demanding more of her than she can give, and she does not believe she can deal with it, or with tomorrow, or the days after that either. She slowly stands up. In the car, with the seatbelt buckled around her heavy coat, she turns clumsily to look behind her as she backs out of the driveway.

At Joe's she moves with short strides up the sidewalk, balancing herself against the weight of the vacuum cleaner. She doesn't knock, because he may be sleeping still. But he is not. As she pushes open the front door she sees him sitting at the kitchen table, wearing the black turtleneck. He smiles and starts to rise, but instead turns his chair to face her and watches her as, leaving the vacuum cleaner, she goes down the hall and kisses him, noting as she lowers her face his weary pallor and the ghost in his eyes. In spite of that and the taste of mouthwash that tells her he has vomited again, she no longer feels like a fugitive. She doesn't understand this, because the feeling began when she woke beside him and therefore it seems that being with him again would not lift it from her. This confuses and frustrates her: when her feelings enter a terrain she neither controls nor understands she thinks they may take her even further, even into madness. She hugs Joe and tells him she has come to clean his apartment; he protests, but he is pleased.

He follows her to the living room and sits on the couch. But after a while, as she works, he lies down, resting his head on a cushion against the arm of the couch. Quietly he watches her. She watches the path of the vacuum cleaner, the clean swath approaching the layers and fluffs of dust. She feels the touch of his eyes, and what is behind them. When she is finished she moves to the bedroom and again he follows her; he lies on the bed, which he has made. For a while she works in a warm patch of sunlight from the window. She looks out at the bright snow and the woods beyond: the spread and reaching branches of elms and birches and maples and tamaracks are bare; there are pines and hemlocks green in the sun. She almost stops working. Her impulse is to throw herself against the window, cover it with her body, and scream in the impotent rage of grief. But she does not break the rhythm of her work; she continues to push the vacuum cleaner over the carpet, while behind her he watches the push and pull of her arms, the bending of her body, the movement of her legs.

When she has vacuumed and dusted the apartment and cleaned the bathtub and lavatory she drinks coffee at the kitchen table while he sits across from her drinking nothing, then with apology in his voice and eyes he says: 'I called the doctor this morning. He said he'd come see me, but I told him I'd go to the office.'

She puts down her coffee cup.

'I'll drive you.'

He nods. Looking at him, her heart is pierced more deeply and painfully than she had predicted: she knows with all her futile and yearning body that they will never make love again, that last night's rushed and silent love was their last, and that except to pack his toilet articles and books for the final watch in the hospital, he will not return to his apartment she has cleaned.

It is night, she is in her bed again, and now Hank turns to her, his hand moving up her leg, sliding her nightgown upward, and she opens her legs, the old easy opening to the hand that has touched her for ten years; but when the nightgown reaches her hips she does not lift them to allow it to slip farther up her body. She is thinking of this afternoon when the priest came to the room and she had to leave. She nodded at the priest, perhaps spoke to him, but did not see him, would not recognize him if she saw him again, and she left and walked down the corridor to the sunporch and stood at the windows that gave back her reflection, for outside the late afternoon of the day she cleaned Joe's apartment was already dark and the streetlights and the houses across the parking lot were lighted. She smoked while on the hospital bed Joe confessed his sins, told the priest about her, about the two of them, all the slow nights and hurried afternoons, and she felt isolated as she had when, months ago, he had begun to die while, healthy, she loved him.

Since breakfast her only contact with Hank and Sharon was calling a sitter to be waiting when Sharon got home, and calling Hank at the college to tell him she was at the hospital and ask him to feed Sharon. Those two phone calls kept her anchored in herself, but the third set her adrift and she felt that way still on the sunporch: Joe had asked her to, and she had phoned the rectory and told a priest whose name she didn't hear that her friend was dying, that he was an ex-priest, that he wanted to confess and receive communion and the last sacrament. Then she waited on the sunporch while Joe in confession told her goodbye. She felt neither anger nor bitterness but a vulnerability that made her cross her arms over her breasts and draw her sweater closer about her shoulders, though the room was warm. She felt the need to move, to pace the floor, but she could not. She gazed at her reflection in the window without seeing it and gazed at the streetlights and the lighted windows beyond the parking lot and the cars of those who visited without seeing them either, as inside Joe finally confessed to the priest, any priest from any rectory. It did not take long, the confession and communion and the last anointing, not long at all before the priest emerged and walked briskly down the corridor in his black overcoat. Then she went in and sat on the edge of the bed and thought again that tomorrow she must bring flowers, must give to this room scent and spirit, and he took her hand.

'Did he understand everything?' she said.

He smiled. 'I realized he didn't have to. It's something I'd forgotten with all my thinking: it's what ritual is for: nobody has to understand. The knowledge is in the ritual. Anyone can listen to the words. So I just used the simple words.'

'You called us adultery?'

'That's what I called us,' he said, and drew her face down to his chest.

Now she feels that touch more than she feels Hank's, and she reaches down and takes his wrist, stopping the hand, neither squeezing nor pushing, just a slight pressure of resistance and his hand is gone.

'I should be with him,' she says. 'There's a chair in the room where I could sleep. They'd let me: the nurses. It would be a help for them. He's drugged and he's sleeping on his back. He could vomit and drown. Tomorrow night I'll stay there. I'll come home first and cook dinner and stay till Sharon goes to bed. Then I'll go back to the hospital. I'll do that till he dies.'

'I don't want you to.'

She looks at him, then looks away. His hand moves to her leg again, moves up, and when she touches it resisting, it moves away and settles on her breast.

'Don't,' she says. 'I don't want to make love with you.'

'You're grieving.'

His voice is gentle and seductive, then he shifts and tries to embrace her but she pushes with her hands against his chest and closing her eyes she shakes her head.

'Don't,' she says. 'Just please don't. It doesn't mean anything any more. It's my fault too. But it's over, Hank. It's because he's dying, yes—' She opens her eyes and looks past her pushing hands at his face and she feels and shares his pain and dismay; and loving him she closes her eyes. 'But you're dying too. I can feel it in your chest just like I could feel it when I rubbed him when he hurt. And so am I: that's what we lost sight of.'

His chest still leans against her hands, and he grips her shoulders. Then he moves away and lies on his back.

'We'll talk tomorrow,' he says. 'I don't trust this kind of talk at night.'

'It's the best time for it,' she says, and she wants to touch him just once, gently and quickly, his arm or wrist or hand; but she does not.

In late afternoon while snowclouds gather, the priest who yesterday heard Joe's confession and gave him the last sacrament comes with the Eucharist, and this time Edith can stay. By now Hank is teaching his last class of the day and Sharon is home with the sitter. Tonight at dinner Sharon will ask as she did this morning: Is your friend dead yet? Edith has told her his name is Mr. Ritchie but Sharon has never seen him and so cannot put a name on a space in her mind; calling him *your friend* she can imagine Joe existing in the world through the eyes of her mother. At breakfast Hank watched them talking; when Edith looked at him, his eyes shifted to the newspaper.

When the priest knocks and enters, Edith is sitting in a chair at the foot of the bed, a large leather chair, the one she will sleep in tonight; she nearly lowers her eyes, averts her face; yet she looks at him. He glances at her and nods. If he thinks of her as the woman in yesterday's confession there is no sign in his face, which is young: he is in his early thirties. Yet his face looks younger, and there is about it a boyish vulnerability which his seriousness doesn't hide. She guesses that he is easily set off balance, is prone to concern about trifles: that caught making a clumsy remark he will be anxious for the rest of the evening. He does not remove his overcoat, which is open. He moves to the bed, his back to her now, and places a purple stole around his neck. His hands are concealed from her; then they move toward Joe's face, the left hand cupped beneath the right hand which with thumb and forefinger holds the white disc.

'The body of Christ,' he says.

'Amen,' Joe says.

She watches Joe as he closes his eyes and extends his tongue and takes the disc into his mouth. His eyes remain closed; he chews slowly; then he swallows. The priest stands for a moment, watching him. Then with his right palm he touches Joe's forehead, and leaves the room. Edith goes to the bed, sits on its edge, takes Joe's hand and looks at his closed eyes and lips. She wants to hold him hard, feel his ribs against hers, has the urge to fleshless insert her ribs within his, mesh them. Gently she lowers her face to his chest, and he strokes her hair. Still he has not opened his eyes. His stroke on her hair is lighter and slower, and then it stops; his hands rest on her head, and he sleeps. She does not move. She watches as his mouth opens and she listens to the near gurgling of his breath.

She does not move. In her mind she speaks to him, telling him what she is waiting to tell him when he wakes again, what she has been waiting all day to tell him but has not because once she says it to Joe she knows it will be true, as true as it was last night. There are still two months of the cold and early sunsets of winter left, the long season of waiting, and the edges of grief which began last summer when he started to die are far from over, yet she must act: looking now at the yellow roses on the bedside table she is telling Hank goodbye, feeling that goodbye in her womb and heart, a grief that will last, she knows, longer than her grieving for Joe. When the snow is melted from his grave it will be falling still in her soul as it is now while she recalls images and voices of her ten years with Hank and quietly now she weeps, not for Joe or Sharon or Hank, but for herself; and she wishes with all her splintered heart that she and Hank could be as they once were and she longs to touch him, to cry on his broad chest, and with each wish and each image her womb and heart toll their goodbye, forcing her on into the pain that waits for her, so that now she is weeping not quietly but with shuddering sobs she cannot control, and Joe wakes and opens his eyes and touches her wet cheeks and mouth. For a while she lets him do this. Then she stops crying. She kisses him, then wipes her face on the sheet and sits up and smiles at him. Holding his hand and keeping all nuances of fear and grief from her voice, because she wants him to know he has done this for her, and she wants him to be happy about it, she says: 'I'm divorcing Hank.'

He smiles and touches her cheek and she strokes his cool hand.

Andre Dubus was born in 1936 in Lake Charles, Louisiana. He was a Marine Corps captain, a college professor, a Guggenheim Fellow, and a member of the Iowa Writer's Workshop. Celebrated for his mastery of the short story, he received the PEN/Malamud Award, the Jean Stein Award from the American Academy of Arts and Letters, the *Boston Globe's* first annual Lawrence L. Winship Award, and fellowships from the Guggenheim Foundation, the National Endowment for the Arts, and the MacArthur Foundation. Dubus died at his home in Haverhill, Massachusetts, in February 1999.

ADULTERY & OTHER CHOICES
has been set in Janson on a VIP photomechanical composing
system. Janson is an old style face, first issued by Anton Janson
in Leipsic between 1660 and 1687, and is typical of the Low
Country designs broadly disseminated throughout Europe and
the British Isles during the seventeenth century. The VIP ver-
sion of this eminently readable and widely employed typeface
is based upon type cast from the original matrices, now in the
possession of the Stempel Type Foundry in Frankfurt, Ger-
many.